Praise for *Let Me Be Like Water*

'*Let Me Be Like Water* is an
enormously beautiful novel—it talks about the fragility
and joy of living, with grief and beyond grief,
in language that is as poetic as it is powerful. It will
stay with you a long time.'
–Sophie Mackintosh,
author of Man Booker–longlisted *The Water Cure*

'A beautiful reflection on love, grief and friendship.
Witty and profound.'
–Fiona Mozley, author of Man Booker–shortlisted *Elmet*

'Intimate, ruthless, tender: this
book is like medicine for the soul. It will heal
and bring back the light.'
–Nina George, author of *The Little Paris Bookshop*

'*Let Me Be Like Water* is a beautiful,
honest and engaging study of how we are healed
through the grace of others.'
–John Burnside, author of *A Summer of Drowning*

'For anyone who has ever loved and lost,
Let Me Be Like Water dares to linger in the small moments.
A truly unique and profound novel. It stays with you.'
–Sharlene Teo, author of *Ponti*

D0543399

'Radiant and brave. A beautifully crafted
study of loss and the redemptive nature of friendship,
and a powerful reminder of the tendernesses
of love, in all its forms.'
–Kate Howard, author of *The Ornatrix*

'A deeply felt, deeply romantic
novel of fragmentary raw emotion, that flickers
and flares like a nerve exposed.'
**–Barney Norris, author of *Five Rivers
Met on a Wooded Plain***

'Holds you in the familiar place of loss, longing, and
survival. Devastating and beautiful.'
–Chimene Suleyman, author of *Outside Looking On*

'A celebration of life and the regenerative
power of friendship. *Let Me Be Like Water* transcends pain
and comforts; it dances in the sky like a kite.'
**–Denis Thériault, author of
*The Peculiar Life of a Lonely Postman***

Let
Me Be
Like
Water

David Higham Associates
FILE COPY
Publication Date: 4 Apr 2019

Let Me Be Like Water

S.K. Perry

🏠 MELVILLE HOUSE
BROOKLYN • LONDON

Let Me Be Like Water

First published in Great Britain in 2018 by

Melville House UK
Suite 2000
16/18 Woodford Road
London
E7 0HA

mhpbooks.com @melvillehouse

Copyright © 2018 by S. K. Perry

First hardback edition: May 2018
First paperback edition: April 2019

The right of S. K. Perry to be identified as the author of this work has been
asserted by her in accordance with the Copyright, Design and Patents Act 1988

A CIP catalogue record for this book is available from the British Library

ISBN: 978-1-911545-25-5
ISBN: 978-1-9115451-3-2 (hardback)

1 3 5 7 9 10 8 6 4 2

Typeset by Octavo Smith Publishing Services
Cover design: Marina Drukman

All rights reserved. No part of this publication may be reproduced, transmitted,
or stored in a retrieval system, in any form or by any means, without permission
in writing from Melville House UK.

Printed in the UK by TJ International Ltd, Padstow, Cornwall

For Kate and David Perry –
who nurtured my love for stories and the sea,

and taught me to believe in magic.

You are like muscle memory;
a spasm of heart – limbs – lungs
toward the once familiar.
I am resisting rehabilitation
in case I forget.

AKI SCHILZ

Autumn

If you were here still,
I'd curl into your ribcage,
my concave lover.

1

I was sitting on a bench staring at the beach when Frank told me I'd dropped my keys. I was watching this little girl playing with a kite. She was quite a long way away, but she gave me something to look at. I can't give you any details: maybe that her front teeth were missing, or that she had tangled hair. I don't remember what I was thinking about, although I know I was wearing my red gloves.

I'd decided to get up and go, ready to continue walking. I was cold and sore from sitting, and at that precise moment I needed something that wasn't the sea to be in front of me. I was about to stand up when Frank – who I didn't know was Frank at the time – told me I'd dropped my keys.

He'd been watching the girl too, it turned out.

He pointed at the kite.

'I have days where I'd like the wind to take me up like that. Some days it's wanting to escape, I think, but on others, I'd just like to be a kite.'

I smiled. He handed me my keys.

'Thank you. I didn't know I'd dropped them.'

'That's OK. I dropped mine on a train track once, between the door and the platform. They had to be hooked back up again by the man from the ticket office. It turned out his name was Noel and he lived down my road. Funny world. What about you; would you like to be a kite, or would you pick something else?'

2

I stripped our bed the night before I left and sat on the floor while the washing machine spun. I watched the sheets twisting round. The bulge of the bowl made me think of a belly with a baby growing inside it. It hurt so much I thought there must be bruises. I needed to find something to hold that felt like you, so I pushed my fist into my mouth and bit down and cried into my knuckles.

It took me nine days to pack. When I got lonely I'd sit on the floor of the shower with the water switched on. Sometimes I'd feel tired, and I'd put down the jeans or the pants or whatever it was I was trying to put into a suitcase, and I'd slide into our bed. I'd lie still and think about how much I miss you. Other times I'd just cry, and my body would shake in that small way that starlings do when they fly together and their wings shudder like sadness in the sky.

I lay awake for most of the night and thought about the woman who was moving in in the morning. I put my suitcases into a big van, and it drove them from our little place in Hammersmith to the sea.

3

'I'm not sure,' I said. 'Maybe I'd be a yo-yo.'

'That'd be good,' Frank replied. 'Kites get to fly though; a yo-yo would be more like a permanent bungee jump.'

We laughed.

'You were about to get going. Are you walking towards the pier?'

'I thought I'd walk to the sailing club. I like the sound the boats make.'

'Me too: the clinking,' Frank said, and he smiled.

4

I've always loved London, so when I started to hate it I knew I had to leave. I didn't want to lose the feeling the river gives me in the morning – even on mizzly days – dispersing the early light on the Southbank as it waits for the sun to get a couple of centimetres higher; or the way the smell of rain gets in between taxis; or how wet, bitter grass springs up outside offices and in parks; or the glow the city gives me at 5 a.m. when I'm dirty from the night before and edging into the day with dry shampoo and muscles still tight from dancing and smoke. But I heard you everywhere: our residue on pavements and the seats of buses, reminding me of a conversation, a look, a half-hour I'd spent waiting for you, or sitting in the office counting down the conversations until I'd step onto the District line to find you. And I walked past grubby doors with newspaper headlines ringing in my mind, hearing the arguments we would have had about them, dissecting the nitty-gritty until you laughed and pushed me up against a street wall, stopping our debate under a pile of bitty kisses.

And without you, the boating lake, and the pub gardens with their wooden benches and fairy lights, and the wind tunnel when a tube pulls away and you tip on the edge of the tracks, and the lines of commuters in walking queues with frowns, clutching coffee in cardboard cups; they all seemed empty.

5

'I feel like some company and Harris isn't quite cutting it.'

Frank pointed at his dog, who was running across the beach. 'Would you mind if I walk with you?'

His voice sat on the wind like they were friends. He was maybe seventy, I reckoned, and there was something solid about him.

'That would be good,' I replied. 'I thought I wanted to be on my own but I don't think I do anymore.'

'Blame the kite,' he said. 'It's made you feel wistful.'

I thought about you: holding my hand and watching me up in the sky.

6

You were in the middle of the dance floor at a university club night; a song I hadn't heard before was playing, and I'd never seen anyone I wanted to talk to so much. My friend was off snogging the DJ, and I was standing by the bar feeling awkward and wishing I was back in my room with a cup of tea. But then there you were, dancing, covered in sweat – amongst a group of bodies that seemed to take up more room than the club could hold – all spiralling arms and beautiful, grinning eyes.

You were laughing at something a girl had said in your ear and then the song wound down, and you started to head for the bar where I was standing in these stupid shoes that were too tight and which made me feel overdressed and clumsy. You never got to the bar though; the first beats of the next track – I can't remember what it was, some indie anthem with too much electric guitar – sucked you back into the bodies, skanking and laughing.

I didn't see you again that night but I sketched your face on my eyelids as I lay in bed falling asleep.

7

'I often see people sitting in their cars just watching the water,' Frank said. 'It makes me want to climb in there with them. I'm sure most of them are fine, but I always wonder if they're sitting there because they've got no one to be outside with. I don't think people should be alone by the sea.'

'Unless they have some very good music playing.'

Frank laughed. 'Yes. Are you a musician?'

'I don't know what I am.'

'Ah, you're in the best possible position. Would you like a ginger nut?'

He got a packet out of his coat pocket and offered it to me.

8

I didn't think you'd noticed me that night in the club but you told me afterwards you had. I never knew whether you were just saying that because you were being nice. I wonder if I'd been looking the other way, or if we hadn't got on the same number 254 bus from Holloway Road to Whitechapel a week later, we'd have found another place to collide.

I was sitting upstairs and you were behind me. The bus went round a corner a bit too fast and I fell off my seat. You burst out laughing and I turned around and saw you, the man I'd drawn on my eyelids.

'How did you manage to fall over when you were sitting down?'

9

Frank and I start to walk. The sea is the colour of pigeons. I can smell September in the sky: leafy and salty and ripe. Two seagulls are bickering over something they've found on the stony slope down to the sea and they hoot at each other before taking off.

I ask Frank if he lives here. He tells me he does, that he's a retired magician, and when he and his partner Ian stopped working they'd moved to the coast.

'What kind of magic do you do?' I ask.

'All kinds,' he says, and he smiles. 'These days I earn a bit of money baking cakes for a friend's coffee shop. Her name's Jackie; you'll meet her soon enough I'm sure. You can smell her shop three miles away so everyone gets sucked in sooner or later.'

Then he pulls a £10 note out from behind my ear and laughs at my surprise.

10

I don't know if you'll remember this, but one of the first times we hung out I was working, I only had an hour free at midday, so you came to see me and said you'd bring lunch. We met in the little park in Stratford and all you'd brought was chocolate cake. There were no sandwiches but you had paper plates and plastic cutlery and little napkins and I laughed, and you didn't understand why I was laughing because you didn't know how else anyone would eat cake except with a fork.

You'd only just moved back here from Paris and you called the cake '*gâteau*', and your voice curled around your words like you were cradling them.

I think about that, four years later, when we share a bed and a flat and you curl round me, squeezing into my knees and the small of my back the same way your accent holds your words, the same way that books made of leather squash into the shape of the bookshelf they sit on.

After we'd eaten you took a kite from your pocket. You unravelled it slowly and we watched it climb into the sky. I remember feeling it tug on my hand, jerking like it didn't know which way to fly. You had the night sky in your eyes: somewhere between navy and black, and you said we should let it go and we did, and it took off over the grey buildings like a firework.

You kissed me then, and I walked you back to the underground and watched you slide through the ticket barrier to the

Jubilee line. You walked away, not looking back, like you knew exactly where you needed to be. You texted me later: *Where do you think our kite got to, Holly? Let's go looking for it soon.*

11

'You've just moved here?' Frank asks.

'Yeah, two weeks ago; I'm staying in Kemptown.'

'Ah, excellent. You can join our book club. We've been hoping for a new member.'

Frank asks how long I'll be around for and I say I don't know. He says he hopes I'll stay long enough to learn to bake. I tell him I don't make cakes but I do like eating them, and I ask him what he thinks about cutlery when doing so. He says fork or no fork, as long as you leave it in your mouth long enough to taste it, it doesn't matter.

The water is very still despite the wind; the waves aren't breaking, just rippling in and dimpling the surface of the sea like bark. I don't know what to make of Frank; he asks me questions like he cares a lot about the answers. He tells me that the book club meet every month to discuss a different book and eat together. He asks me if I've read *Narcopolis*; I haven't but he says I can borrow his copy and if I read a bit I can come to their next meeting on the Wednesday coming. That his friend Gabriella will be cooking and it will be unmissable. That there will be cutlery but it won't be obligatory. We both laugh at that.

I'm glad to get out of my head for a while; his voice is a relief. He speaks slowly, letting the air fill the gaps in our conversation and laughing at all his own jokes. Soon we are past the old pier and the boats, and we stop for some cider in a little pub on the seafront that turns into a club at night.

He tells me that on a Thursday he hosts a drawing class he used to go to until he realised he couldn't draw at all. I tell him everyone can draw, they just need to practise, and he says that's probably true but he prefers to knit, which is also very useful because you can never have enough socks.

'I started when Ian died. I'd sit in the evenings and the room would be so quiet. I thought about how sad he'd feel to know I was just sitting there missing his noise in the room. Knitting needles make this sound, clinking together, and it made me feel like he was chatting to me. I think it's why I like the noise the boats make so much; it's similar; it's like they have something to say.'

'How long ago did he die?' I ask.

'Six years. Do you know, he is still the only person who made no sense to me at all the first time I met him. Completely haphazard.' He laughs. 'But he had red hair and he walked assertively, and he liked to drink tea in thin, cold china cups. I didn't have a choice but to be with him in the end.'

I want to tell him about you but the words feel like cement in my mouth. Frank looks me straight in the eyes. It's disconcerting, from a stranger. I ask something vague about him being a magician. He says it's the best job in the world but that anyone can do magic and he can tell I have it in me.

He tells me to open my hand, I do and there's a flower in it, and I shake my head and ask him how he did it. He says that it was me, and I really shouldn't feel sad when I can make flowers grow out of thin air. I don't ask him how he knows I'm sad; I just slip the flower into my bag and listen to the water swaying. 'Anyway,' he says, 'when you're by the sea everything works out alright.'

12

There are seagulls playing in the waves. It's 2 a.m. and I'm sitting on the beach looking at the sea. The birds dart around and the night makes them glow like the round bits in Pac-Man. And I just stand there and I shout. And I don't know if you can hear me, Sam, but if I don't try to talk to you I'm scared my tongue will stop working and I'll forget how to move my bones. I'm scared my skin will forget how to feel anything at all without your hands on my spine while I sleep.

13

A week after the date in the park you're sitting on my bed. We'd been out to dinner; we ate Mexican food with our fingers. You'd told me about growing up in Cameroon and moving to be with your dad in London and then university in Paris. Now you're studying in London again. We've got guacamole and chilli in our fingernails. I've told you I grew up on the edge of the city, that I still feel like I'm growing up now. I've looked at your hands moving to your mouth, and at your mouth, and we know that none of this stuff matters anyway, that we've known each other all along.

You tell me you've never seen anyone you wanted to talk to so much as you did when I fell off my seat on the bus. I tell you that although I'm studying philosophy, I want to write songs. You tell me how hard you find it being the son of your father. I tell you I like how you dance, although I don't like indie nights and you shake your head at me and laugh. We walk home holding hands. Now I'm lying down next to where you're sat and you say, 'Sing me a song.'

'What? No.'

'Please, sing me something. I want to hear you sing.'

You lie back on the bed next to me. We face each other and I look into your sky-eyes.

You say, 'If you sing, I'll sing.'

I laugh at you.

'What are you talking about? I don't want you to sing.'

'You want to be a singer; why are you so afraid to do what you do? You're gorgeous too. Are you afraid of that?'

I can't hold eye contact but you put your hand on my hip as I look down and you move my chin up with your other hand and kiss me. There's chilli on my tongue.

'Tomorrow,' I say. 'I'll sing to you tomorrow, maybe. Let's do this for now.'

I put my feet on yours and move in closer so our whole bodies are touching. When you breathe out, I breathe you in. The skin on my lips brushes yours and you pull me closer, move your hands under my jumper and hold the cradle of my back. I'm scared by how quickly I become part of you.

14

Frank and I arrange to meet the next day by New Steine Gardens so he can lend me *Narcopolis*. He's waiting there with Harris when I arrive. It's drizzling and the memorial statue splits the sky like broken wings. Frank has a flask of tea and he pours me a cup and hands me a ginger nut. We decide to walk along the front for a bit. The rain is heavier now but he tells me there's no point living by the sea if you don't like getting wet and I laugh and zip up my mac.

We go down the steps to Madeira Drive. The railings are the same kind of green as hospital overalls so I look at the water instead. It's moving slowly, like the extra wetness in the sky gives weight to its rhythm. I take Harris's lead from Frank and let him pull me along. When Frank lets him off to run ahead, the wind carries me instead. *Little kite.*

'Is there anywhere you need to be today?' Frank asks.

'I don't think so.'

'I was hoping you'd say that. I'm going to walk to Ovingdean for some cake. I've always found that cake in the rain is surprisingly good. Do you want to come?'

On the beach the stones shine like wet skin. It's good to feel joined to something; when I breathe out, my sadness feels like part of the rain. I like cake, so I nod. Frank points at the ground and bends down to pick something up.

'Look,' he says. 'A yo-yo. It must have been there waiting for you.'

15

About a month after the Mexican food I come to your house for dinner. It's a Thursday evening. You live forty-five minutes west on the District line. It's dark and I'm cold when I arrive, so you give me a blanket to sit in while you cook. In the kitchen you're frenetic, chucking ingredients into the pan and making all your movements bigger than they need to be. Your housemates congregate round the table and you put the music on loud so we're all laughing over it.

We've been exploring each other quickly. Tonight we are the opposite sides of a compass, looking across at each other as the room whirls around us. Other times, I've been the needle and you've been north: holding me there with nothing between us, not even a breath apart.

You pan fry us fish in a kind of peanut paste with lime. I'm held by the noise of the oil spitting and your friends talking over the drum beats. Whenever you walk past me to get something from the cupboard or to chuck something in the sink, your hands brush across my shoulders.

Later, my tongue brushes over your thighs and you tell me that you love me. You say it in French and Yemba and English. *Je t'aime. Je t'adore mon petit cerf-volant.*

16

Frank and I walk through the marina complex to the cliffs on the other side, where there's a flat, wide walkway. The tide is in, banging against the wall where the path drops away to the sea. The waves spray up onto it, tearing themselves apart on the concrete. The energy of it makes me want to run, or roller-skate, or do something fast. We look at each other and laugh. Frank picks up a stone and hurls it into the water. I do the same and we keep going until we've run out of things to throw, and then we walk, dodging the waves as they rush in.

After a mile or so we find the cake shop – a counter cut into the side of the cliff – where we buy banana bread and Victoria sponge. We rest on the wall and look out across the sea.

'How you doing over there, Holly?' he asks.

'I'm thinking I need to get a job. I can't just eat cake and wander round all day.'

He laughs.

'You'll find something. That stuff always slips into place. Anyway, look at the rain,' he says. 'Sometimes falling for a bit is the right thing to do.'

He puts his palm out to catch the rain and closes his hand around a few drops of water. When he opens it again there's a little piece of paper folded inside. I take it and read what it says inside: *Go gently*. I look at Frank but he shrugs, 'Don't ask me; it fell from the sky.'

17

Six months after the park date we're at your house again. We're running late for your friend's engagement party and you're making a speech. You're tense because you don't like public speaking and you can't decide whether to wear your dinner jacket or your kaftan.

I say, 'Sam, you would look amazing in a bin bag. Please put something on and let us leave.'

You snap at me.

'That's not very helpful is it, Holly? I obviously can't wear a bin bag.'

You're being ridiculous and it makes me love you even more. I don't tell you this. I laugh instead and move into your body and put my arms around your waist, my head resting just under your chin.

'You'll be so good tonight. Please, stop worrying.'

You are hot, tense. Your muscles relax as I lean my body into you and we breathe together.

I say, 'Wear the kaftan. I'll make you a cup of tea for the taxi; it'll calm you down.'

'Oh really. And spill it all down me? Take a mug into the party?'

'We'll give it to the driver.'

You laugh.

'Go away, you little weirdo; I need to finish up.'

18

On Wednesday it's the book club and I'm nervous; I've only got through the first few chapters and I don't know what to expect of the other people who'll be there. I arrive first but Frank has told Gabriella I'll be coming and she shows me into her kitchen. It's thick with coriander and root vegetables and I say something about how good it smells.

'I know, it does, doesn't it,' Gabriella says. 'It's a new recipe and I'm pretty pleased with it. Tea? Wine?'

'Tea, please.'

She pours me a cup from a thick brown teapot and passes me the milk.

'Sugar?'

'No, thanks.'

She adds three teaspoons to hers.

'Frank tells me you've just moved here?'

'Yeah, from London. About three weeks ago now.'

The walls of her kitchen are red, like the inside of a stomach.

'I commute to London every day for work; it's a pain but it's worth it not to live there.'

I think about your mum moving to York, her wanting to get out of the city too.

'What do you do?' I ask.

'I trained as a dancer,' Gabriella says. 'But I did a masters in theatre production and now I work in film. So, bits of everything really.'

Gabriella looks like a dancer. She's tall and compact. Her words are precise and soft, her accent clipped like Radio 4. She will tell me later that her parents were from Tobago but she's lived here her whole life. She grew up in Birmingham but she doesn't have a Brummy twang. She says they wouldn't let her pick one up, and she spent hours listening to the BBC trying to learn the right way to speak.

'Did you move to Brighton for work?' she asks.

I don't have an answer ready so I kind of shrug.

'Why did you?'

'I took my son to London when he was eight. We were living in Birmingham and we caught the train in to go to the Natural History Museum. We went down to the river afterwards and stood on Tower Bridge for a picture. After I took it, he turned to me with a bogey on his finger and asked why his snot turned black in London. I decided then and there that I wouldn't live in a place where pollution turns your insides dirty.'

I laugh. 'So you moved to Brighton?'

'Yeah, we moved to Brighton. About nine years ago now. We'd only been here a few months when he got leukaemia. He died six months later.'

I look at her, remembering to breathe. It's what you do when you're still alive; I know this.

'His name was Joseph. He was the one who taught me how to cook. He wanted to be a chef his whole life and at the weekends he'd spend hours making up recipes. I'd put the radio on in the kitchen and chop vegetables for him and talk to him about films and school and just things we thought about. He wrote down all the recipes in a big folder that tied together with a ribbon and we covered it in handmade paper. When he died I used to sleep with that book under my pillow.'

'I'm so sorry, Gabriella.'

'I felt like someone had pressed pause, like I might never move again,' she says. 'I'd go for these long walks and sip tea in plastic cups from takeaway shops. I wouldn't go in the kitchen. I ate cold ready meals in our guest bedroom and drank water from the bathroom tap. Then – not long after the funeral – I just came in here, and turned on the radio and started cooking. I took out his recipe book and opened it on the first page and rolled up my sleeves, and I chopped and grilled and seared and fried and seasoned and sobbed for my little boy, and when I had finished sobbing I carried on cooking.'

My eyes are watery.

'I'm no good at cooking,' I say.

She smiles and passes me a tissue from a box next to the hob. The doorbell rings and she looks at me.

'Oh dear, the others are coming. Are you alright if I get that?'

I nod. She squeezes my hand and says,

'If you come here on a Sunday, I'll teach you. See if you want to after you've tried the stew tonight.'

19

Your mum only speaks French and Yemba at home, you've told me; she doesn't like speaking English because of your dad. He'd lived here for so long he spoke it perfectly, but she found the language hard. It was one of the things she'd felt had never been enough for him.

'That stuff won't matter with you,' you say. 'She knows how much you mean to me. Just be yourself.'

We're on the tube on our way there, and I'm nervous. It's the overground bit of the underground and normally you'd make a joke about that, but you keep giving me advice about how to be normal, which makes me feel even more uptight.

We snap at each other. I fiddle with my scarf and look out of the window at the trees. They're the colour of berries and lipstick and rust.

'*Ne te stresses pas*, Holly.'

'What?'

'Relax. It's not a test.'

'Oh please, you're hardly relaxed, are you?'

There's silence. I'm anxious about meeting your family. You know this and it makes you angry.

'You're making this a big thing, and it isn't.'

'I'm making it a big thing? We've been together for a year and it's the first time you've taken me home.'

'Don't be a bitch, Holly. *Arrêtes*. We've talked about this; she's religious and I needed to be sure we were serious. Why do we have to have this conversation again?'

You stand up and I watch you walk away down the carriage. You wait by the doors and at Dollis Hill you get off the tube. I let you go but when the doors close I don't feel angry anymore; I feel sick.

The tube starts to slow down again and I can feel my pulse fighting with it; I need to get off too. At the next stop the doors open and I swap to the other side of the platform. The adrenaline's making it hard for me to stand up; my muscles are tight and panicky. The southbound tube arrives and I get on and close my eyes. At Dollis Hill you're still sat on the platform.

'Forget it,' you say. 'If it's such an awful thing let's not even go.'

'I'm sorry, Sam.'

'Fuck it, Holly, let's just not do it.'

'I'm sorry. I'm sorry. I really want to meet them.'

A train pulls in, heading north.

'*Si te plaît, Sam, on y va. Je veux vraiment y aller.*'

You stand up, and we get on the tube in silence. Your eyes are wet. We're still fighting but I take your hand and hold it so tightly you tell me it hurts.

'Please don't cry,' I say. 'Don't ever cry because of me.'

I think about this fight when I sit on my bed at night looking out at the sea, unable to sleep. I feel stupid for asking such a ridiculous thing of you. I want to pummel you with my fists; I want to see you bruise.

20

Gabriella's stew tastes like home. It doesn't taste like a home I've lived in yet; it's a home in Tobago by the beach. It's warm from the oven and warm all the way through: an initial sting of chilli, overtones of coriander, the infusion of ginger and nutmeg that sears the through the vegetables, the earthiness of cumin and something I can't identify. Cinnamon, maybe.

It's loaded with pulses and beans and vegetables from Gabriella's garden, and rich tomato juices that seem thicker than passata and fresher than purée, with tiny lumps of cheese that somehow escape melting and stand firm against the other flavours, like little pockets of punch. And then almonds, which Gabriella tells me she fries right at the start with the onions and the spices; they absorb the oil and taste like crunchy sweets, packed with swirling tastes distinct from the liquids of the dish. She adds in a twist of coconut milk, lifting the heat with its creamy sweetness, and serves the finished dish with baby spinach leaves and fried, crispy plantain.

21

We wake up already tangled in each other. It's Sunday and I'm hungover and I've been in love with you for more than a year. You make us spiced eggs. We eat them in your bed with coffee and Bloody Marys. You've added so much Tabasco I choke on mine and you laugh at me. We sit in bed all day, you editing your thesis, me writing songs.

22

There are seven members of the book club, including me, Frank and Gabriella. The others are Ellie, Noel, Danny and Jackie. Jackie is the one who owns the cafe where Frank's cakes go, and I think Noel is the man from the train station who rescued his keys. Ellie and Danny are both my age, or maybe a bit older.

Danny really likes *Narcopolis* but Jackie doesn't. She laughs at him because he keeps trying to persuade her it's brilliant and she doesn't agree. Frank asks Noel to read a bit aloud and everyone finds it funny. I don't really get it but they're all so happy it's infectious.

We're clearing the plates away, ready to go home, when Ellie corners me.

'Me and Danny are going to the pub now. You should come. You need to help us to keep the excitement going after all these fuddy-duddies hit the hay.'

Jackie smiles. 'It's true, Holly; these two must be delighted Frank's recruited someone still young enough to get tiddly on a Wednesday night. Don't let them down.'

I laugh.

'Why not?'

I look around at the others, all putting on their shoes and coats. Frank seems to hold everyone together, like they're the leaves and he's the branch, and no one wants it to be winter. As I leave he smiles at me.

'You need to be more careful with your keys, Holly.'

'What do you mean? They're in my pocket.'

I look for them but they're not there. Frank pulls them out of the air behind me and passes them back with a wink. I shake my head at him and we laugh.

Ellie, Danny and I leave together. It's a cold night and it feels thick, like any moment the sky will crack again and pour with rain. I notice the air more now I'm not in London. It chafes my ankles between my socks and jeans and I sink my hands into my coat pockets to get warm. In my left pocket I find an old apple core I can't remember putting there. I try to sneak it out but Ellie catches me and cackles as I go to flick it in the bin.

'That's really grim, Holly. How long has that been there?'

I throw it at her instead and we run laughing down the road.

23

I keep your big red cashmere jumper bundled up on the chair by my bed. I sleep in it every night. It makes me too hot.

24

We head into North Laine and duck into a pub. It smells of prawn crackers and there's an open-mic night going on. Danny buys a bottle of red wine and some peanuts, and we sit at a table in the corner. Danny is tall, white and skinny, with eyebrows that really commit to his face. They move when he talks. He jiggles his leg under the table as he tells me he works for a record label with Ellie's boyfriend, designing artwork for album covers. Ellie's doing a PhD in neuroscience, and Danny asks her how it's going. She turns to me, smiling.

'He knows everything there is to know about music but try talking to him about acetylcholine and the basal ganglia and he's completely useless. I don't know why he's bothering to ask.'

'Shame,' I reply. 'I really struggle with people who can't talk about ganglias.'

Danny chucks a peanut at her head.

'I'm being polite, Eleanor. You ever heard of social niceties?'

Ellie laughs and gets out a pack of cigarettes, 'Do you smoke?'

'Thanks. I have rollies.'

We go outside, leaving Danny to guard the wine.

Ellie lights up and leans on the pub wall, breathing the smoke out in perfect rings. She turns to me and says, 'Disgusting habit. We should quit. So what do you do; do you have a job down here?'

'Sort of. I joined a cleaning agency; I have a trial shift on Friday. I put an ad up in the newsagent too, saying I could teach piano. I have an interview at the weekend.'

'Cool. Do you sing as well as play?'

'Yeah. It used to be what I wanted to do but now I don't really know. Things are a bit up in the air.'

'The open mic here happens every week. We should come back. I bet you sound great; you've got a really sultry speaking voice; I noticed when you were talking about the book.'

I laugh at her and choke on my smoke.

'Not so sultry now, darling,' she says, going cross-eyed and whacking me on the back. 'Get some wine in you quick; we need to lubricate that throat.'

She stomps our cigarettes out and pushes me back inside the pub.

'Quick, Danny, she's dying. For Christ's sake, give the girl some more vino rosso pronto, or we'll never see her round these parts again.'

25

I just want you to be here.

26

We get through the wine pretty quickly and the first bottle becomes a second. The open-mic night is winding down and

Danny decides we should play darts so Ellie says she'll take us both on. He and I make a pretty good team but Ellie keeps missing the board completely. She blames the music.

'I'm telling you, I know about these things. The rhythms in the stuff they play here just don't provide a suitable environment for effective motor-neurone activity. You two must have some pretty weird brains to be doing so well.'

We laugh and abandon the game. We sit in the corner and talk about nothing, staying until closing. Outside I feel kind of warm, but the ground looks syrupy under the shine of the streetlamps and it's raining again. It seems later than 11.30.

Danny hails a taxi.

'We'll do the rounds,' he says. 'Where do you need to go to, Holly?'

I'm the only one going east so they drop me off first, on the corner of Upper Rock Gardens. The lights are out in the house I'm staying in, and I don't feel like going inside yet. There's no colour on the walls of my room; it's no one's fault but it makes me angry. There's a patch behind the bed where I've been peeling the wallpaper off when I can't sleep. I feel guilty but it's easier than screaming; it doesn't wake anyone up.

I'm hungry now and I think about the apple core that was in my pocket. I want to eat. I remember seeing a kebab shop down the road; it was pink, with a man with a bird on his head painted on the wall. I don't know what I'd order if I go there though; I'm tired. It's still raining and I need to make a decision so I stand in the doorway of the church on the corner for shelter.

I think about phoning my parents but it's late and I don't

know what to say. *My socks are wet. I got some flowers for my room but I didn't put them in water so they died. I feel so lonely. There are four days left this week and it's been raining a lot. I've stopped brushing my hair but I think it looks alright. Every part of my body hurts. I don't want you to tell me you love me.*

That night I dream of brains that chase me out into the middle of road, and the sound of brakes and crumpling metal and the smell of burning.

27

I get a piano teaching job. It's every Saturday with a little girl who's about to turn eight and is working towards Grade 3. Her last teacher moved to Berlin, her mother tells me.

'You're not planning to do that, are you? It's just terribly difficult for Louisa; she builds up such strong attachments.'

I assure her I'm not, and she gives me the job.

28

I can see you dancing from where I'm singing on the stage. It's the first gig of mine you've been to and I thought it would make me nervous but I'd forgotten what you're like when you dance. You're in a big crowd with the rest of our friends and sometimes you sink into them but I can sense you feeling the beat with me and it makes me better. I move to the piano for the next song; it's slower, and I get lost in it so when the set's finished and I walk down from the stage, I'm surprised to see you there ready to wrap me up.

We sit – a group of us – at the bar while the next band

sets up and then we dance together until we ache. You look so good when you're dancing, and you make everyone round us seem better than they are. You feel music in the same place that makes me want to play it and you spin me round like the whole room was built for us to move in.

I can feel the moisture already drying in my bra as we leave and the autumn air hits us. It's dark and cold outside, and you push me up against the wall and take a handful of my hair and kiss me.

'I'm so proud of you, little kite. Dancing to your voice is almost as good as waking up next to you in the morning.'

We walk home that night; it takes over an hour but we want to be outside. You say you can't imagine standing still on a bus. Whenever there's something to crash into we do; we let the streets' walls hold us up and our mouths open round each other.

At home you push me into the door as I close it. You kiss me, your head nuzzled into the back of my neck. I turn round to face you and you lift me up and I wrap my legs around your waist. You try to take my top off but you can't balance me at the same time. You put me down again and we take off our own clothes. We both try to do it quickly, and it's kind of funny. I'm naked first. It's a bit cold and I watch you take your socks off and then we're both there, standing with our clothes next to us. You smile at me and I laugh. You put your arms around me and we kiss.

'Where are we going?' I ask.

'I don't know. The floor?'

We lie down facing each other. I put my leg up over your

thigh and you push your hips forward and move into me. You hook your arm under my leg and use your hand too, and I curl close into your body. We move like that, and I hold onto your back and push my fingers into your shoulder blades, curling them around you like the bend in a river. I don't close my eyes. You find my hand and we hold on, hanging together, moving through the space that's between us until there's nothing there, and we only exist like water.

29

It's suddenly Sunday again. It's been raining for forty-eight hours and where I'm sat on the beach it feels like it will never be dry again. The stones are all different colours and I wish I knew more about why. This is the kind of thing I would ask you. Instead I throw them into the sea, as hard and as far as I can, over and over again. I stand up to do it. I know you can wish on stones, so I hurl them into the sea wishing for things like an end to global warming and new trainers and you.

I'm glad it's raining because it means there's no one outside to see me. I'm making strange guttural noises every time I throw a stone. It's making my throat sore but the stones don't break when I throw them and I want something to hurt. I sound like a tennis player at Wimbledon. Or someone with terrible constipation. This thought makes me laugh and then I can't stop laughing, and my knees bend as my stomach starts to ache and I lie on the ground laughing and laughing at the horizon and the rain clouds and the strange little woman shouting and hurling rocks into the sea.

Back in my room I put on dry clothes. It's not even lunch-time yet but I think about getting into bed, letting the day roll into the night in sleep. Then I get a text from Frank saying he's going to take the car down towards Haywards Heath, for a walk by the viaduct at Balcombe, and do I want to come too.

30

You found it frustrating how hard I found it to drive, and how complicated I made maths. These are things I'm trying to fix. We fought – me fierce, you more amused – over the Monty Hall Problem, the one where you're on a game show and you're offered the choice of three doors. You know that behind one door is a car, and if you pick the right door you'll win it. But behind the other two there are goats. So, say you pick a door, maybe No. 1, and then the host, who knows what's behind all the doors, opens another one, let's say No. 3, and this door is one of the ones with a goat. The host then asks you if you want to change to door No. 2, and the Monty Hall Problem is whether or not you're more likely to win if you switch doors, or keep it the same.

31

During my first ever driving lesson I was so nervous I couldn't breathe, and I had to keep stopping for little air breaks. I'd drive a bit and then I'd pull over to take some breaths before getting going again. The first time I tried driving round a roundabout I was so nervous about stalling I concentrated everything on the clutch and the gear stick and completely forgot to steer, so I just drove straight into it.

You found this ridiculous. You told me you didn't understand how someone so steady on their feet could be so dangerous in a car.

You told me you liked the fact I'm dangerous. We'd laugh and find ways of making our bodies move even closer together.

32

That day, on the way to Balcombe, Frank tells me driving is just mind over matter so he gets me to drive the country lane part, after we're off the main roads. We wind down the windows and he puts Bob Marley on at full volume.

I ask him what to do about L-plates and he shouts back over the music that no one should ever stop being a learner and it's a stupid distinction to make. He tells me to put my foot down and relax. He flicks his chair back and starts to sing along in a booming bass as I turn the key. 'Just don't tap your foot along,' he says. 'And if you see a roundabout, try not to drive through it; the clue's in the name.'

I haven't told him about the roundabout I drove into. But I haven't told him about you either, and when we arrive at the viaduct he says, 'You drove well, Holly. You're fixing it.'

33

I said I'd stick to my guns: stick with the door I'd chosen in the first place and see the decision through. You said it wasn't a matter of commitment but of probability and I'd have more of a chance of winning the car if I switched.

I said that if there was a one-in-three chance of all the doors having a car behind them and the car doesn't move, then just because one of the other doors doesn't have a car behind it, doesn't make it more or less likely for the one I'd picked in the first place to be right? I said that it didn't make sense because nothing's changed; we already knew that one of the doors we didn't pick had a goat behind it, and now all that's happened is we've seen the spare goat, which we'd already known about anyway.

And I was really angry that you couldn't make me understand why you'd switch doors. You even started telling me a theory someone had made up about a little green woman. You wanted to prove the point that I was making to disprove your point, because you wanted to show me that what I was saying actually proved that you were right. And I didn't know what you were on about and I wanted you to draw a probability tree to help me understand, and you started laughing at me and that made me even angrier; and I told you that I hate not understanding things – like how everyone expects you to use pi all the time, as though it shouldn't even matter to you that they can't possibly know for sure that it goes on and on forever without repeating itself, because if it does go on and on forever they couldn't possibly have seen all the way to the end and checked that it never repeated, and if it does go on and on forever then how can they also know that it's the exact right number to do all the sums with circles with – and you were laughing even more now, which made me even more enraged. Then you asked me exactly who it was that wanted me to use pi all the time, and told me I was just getting cross because you'd told me I'd end up with a goat and not a car, and I told you that I couldn't even drive anyway so I couldn't care less about whether I got a goat or not, that I don't like how cars smell of metal and moths, and that I was just annoyed because it didn't make sense, and that you had to know you couldn't just tell me things if you couldn't explain to me why they were true.

34

Frank told me the viaduct was made of 11 million bricks and opened in the summer of 1841. The bricks were imported from Holland and shipped up the River Ouse, and then a team of people slotted all 11 million of them together to build the tumble of arches we were walking under. He said he'd always liked magic because it was one of the few things that made people happier when they didn't understand it. That coming to a viaduct constructed from 11 million bricks made him feel how he hoped other people did when he made things float in the air.

As we turned our backs on the viaduct and started our walk back to the car, Frank stopped.

'I wish I knew the name of one of the builders,' he said. 'It's such a shame they weren't able to sign it or something; they spent so long building it. Do you think one of them might have been called Edward?'

'I think Edward is a strong possibility.'

'Me too,' Frank replied. 'I think I'd like to thank him. What do you reckon?'

'Thank Edward?'

'Yes.'

And then louder, 'Thank you, Edward; I think you're great. We think you're really great for building this viaduct. Hello, Edward!'

I joined in.

'Hello, Edward! Thank you! Thank you, Edward!'

We must have stood there for two or three minutes, laughing, with Harris running around us in figures of eight and barking, and us calling backwards for two hundred years to a man who may or may not have been called Edward. We tried out a bunch of other names too, all vaguely Victorian. Frank started to dance: waving and sort of jumping and whooping, 'Thank you, Edward! Thank you, Archibald!' at the sky and the bridge. I joined in, spinning around on the spot and whirling my arms until I was dizzy from moving and breathing and shouting.

'You're not driving home,' Frank muttered when we'd stopped and were standing still again, listening to Harris and to each other, panting. 'You're clearly erratic and dangerous. I think it's best if we let Harris drive so that we're free to yell at strangers through the windows.'

'I think that's probably wise. He looks like the kind of dog who could get us home safe.'

Darkness was closing in, and as we walked back to the car Frank started to sing again. I started running a bit with Harris, jumping around and dancing. A passerby going the other direction went past us with a nervous grin as Frank waved and sang at her. I jumped up a little too eagerly and slid over in a patch of mud. I pushed myself back up and Harris rushed over. I looked at Frank and started to cry. He walked over quickly.

'It's OK, Holly,' he said, and put a hand on my shoulder. 'Do you want a ginger nut?'

He started to get the packet out of his pocket but I shrugged him off and shook my head.

'I don't want a biscuit, Frank.'

I wanted to be a long way away from him. This strange man, with his cakes and his dog and his collection of broken people, who knew more about me than I'd told him. I needed to be away from everyone.

'I want you to leave me alone,' I said.

He looked at me.

'Shout it,' he replied.

'What?'

'Shout it; "I want you to leave me alone," as loud as you can.'

'What are you talking about?'

I wanted to hurt something; I was full of you, full of something, shaking.

'I want you to leave me alone,' he shouted. 'I want you to leave me alone.'

'Leave me alone!' I shouted it back, and then again and again up out of my body and I was crying and shouting and I needed the pain to stop.

'Leave me alone! Leave me alone! Leave me alone!'

Then I was just hungry, and tired, with nothing else to say.

'Better?' Frank handed me a hanky. 'Come on, let's go back to the car; you'll feel OK in the warm. Let's get you home.'

'I'm so sorry, Frank,' I said and I turned to him, and remembered he was kind and had bought me banana bread and was helping me make friends.

'Don't apologise, Holly. Rage is healthy. You've got to let it out.'

He offered me the ginger nuts again and I accepted one, and he took my arm as we walked back to the car.

'Where did you come from, Frank?' I asked. 'How do you know so much?'

'I've been here all along,' he replied. 'I'm a magician.'

35

Danny texted me in the week to see if I wanted to join him and Ellie for a pub quiz: *It's on Wednesday at the Sidewinder right by your house. We're going to the St James before for Thai food and rum. See you there?*

I had two houses booked in for cleaning and a piano lesson in the evening. Rum sounded good. About ten minutes after I'd said yes I got a text from Ellie: *Heard Danny invited you to quiz. Need your best fun fact before you get my approval. Make it a good one. Ellie x*

I replied: *The longest recorded flight of a chicken was 13 seconds and 301.5 feet long. Hope you'll have me, my general knowledge is not what it could be but I'm a solid team player.*

She came back to me straight away: *Chicken-based facts are my favourite. See you there at 7.30 x*

36

One of the houses I clean is filled with china ornaments: all pastoral scenes with inane grinning animals. They sit on rows of shelves that line the hallway and the stairs. It takes me an hour to dust them, and they smile at me like they know how obscene I find them. There's one – a particularly perky shepherdess in a blue frilly skirt and bonnet – that gets to me more than the others. She's trivial, and she puts on this glazed-over smirk to taunt me. Today, when I get to her shelf, I hurl her at the floor. She smashes instantly. It's satisfying, and I think about smashing them all.

Later on – when the owner of the house comes home – I apologise; I tell her it was an accident and offer to pay. Then I hoover it all up and go home.

When I get back to my room there is a packet of ginger nuts on my bed with a handwritten note. *Go gently H*. When I turn it over there's a picture of a sheep on the front. The sheep looks pretty grumpy though, which is a relief. I laugh. I guess Frank finds chirpy farmyard scenes irritating too, but that's the only part of it I can make sense of.

37

The first night at the book club was the first time I'd seen someone as thin as Ellie. Her fingers were like twigs and where her knuckles made them a little wider her skin was saggy and dried, as though this was the only place on her body where there was any excess. Her clothes were all too big and her hair was falling out slightly in places where the skin on her scalp was too fragile to anchor in the follicles. She looked like a cross between a bird that had just been born and an old lady, and you could see the hunger cramps and the resilience and the pain cutting into her eyes and her skin as soon as you looked at her. I think that's why I was so surprised by how funny she was, and when she'd sit shivering from the cold of not eating while arguing vehemently about international development policy or the relevance of twentieth-century French philosophy to modern-day Marxism, I'd wonder how it could be the same mind that drove these different sides of her, and how someone so completely dynamic and vital could be living out her own destruction.

38

We came second to bottom in the pub quiz – mostly because we'd saved our joker for the picture round, which turned out to be an error – but also because we'd drunk too much rum.

We know better the following week. Ellie brings a friend from her department at the university: Duane. He is witty, sharp and tells me he loves comic books. He says that some people find it surprising in a Jamaican man, but he enjoys the exposure of social constructs through irrational incongruity. I don't really know what to say to that, so I talk to him about *Doctor Who*. I know that's not the same as comic books but he doesn't seem to mind, and we argue over whether it'd be worse to be stuck on a desert island with a Dalek or a Zygon.

Ellie's boyfriend Sean has a wide, angular face and a voice that slides out gently when he speaks. He's lived in Brighton all his life and met Ellie at school. They're both white, and his accent is less clipped than hers is. He works with Danny and Mira, who they've brought along from the record label. Mira says 'fuck' a lot. She is tall, trendy and acerbic. She sits next to me, taking the piss out of the table next to us who have matching team T-shirts. We decide to get some printed for the week after, and I don't even think she's joking. We rise to a respectable fourth place and feel smug.

After the quiz is done we buy pizzas from the bar and sit for a bit, laughing about the questions we got wrong. Danny buys my pizza for me because I'm out of cash and insists I have to try turkey and ham with Worcester sauce and gherkins. The man behind the bar thinks we're idiots but it tastes better than I expect.

'You see,' he says. 'I know a lot about pizza.'

'Shame you don't know more about current affairs,' Mira says. Danny is indignant.

'You shouldn't be laughing at me, Holly; I just bought you dinner!'

We get pissed, and it's Duane who suggests we walk down to the beach. We get our stuff together and go outside. It's a quiet walk. The town is asleep and the noise of the waves makes the silence feel padded, like we're under the sea or something. I don't know, we're pretty drunk.

On the beach, the big wheel looms up and there's a little bar flashing lasers out onto the stones. To my right the pier glitters. It's only really dark when you look out to sea and – under the surface – it could be hiding anything.

Duane and Mira walk down to the water's edge to paddle and check out the temperature. Soon we're all down there, kicking water at each other and laughing. I don't know who does it first but we pull off our clothes and run in properly, the shock of it wearing down to a numbness, and then I'm floating on my back laughing as Sean tries to pull Ellie in.

I stay like that, trying to hold my body as still as I can. It's dark and I can't see the water around me. When I put my ears under the surface I hear nothing except the rustle of my blood moving round my body. It sounds like someone rolling over between clean, crisp sheets in bed at night. The coast, which has drifted further away is sprinkled with yellow and white, and outwards – to the edge of the sea – there is only heavy, sooty sky. I think about what would happen if I decided to stay here, where the water would wash me to. I feel calm so I breathe all the way out and let my lungs fill back up slowly. I don't need to be anything here; I am held by the salt, and the sea, and the thick, black sky, and none of it minds who I am. I let the sadness in slowly, as the cold eases out of my bones, and my body fills up with everything I've been pushing away. I start to cry, and it makes my body fold, so I roll over onto my front and put my face into the water. I cry straight into it, holding my breath, but then I start to shake so I open my mouth and I choke on the sea. I've lost the thread of the conversation and the others are laughing at a joke I've missed. I push myself deeper under the surface and open my eyes into the sting of it. It's dark inside the water: just empty space and the place in my throat where I choke on memories of you. I am somewhere it hurts to be but it would be such an effort to drown; my body wants so much to keep me up and I'm tired, too tired to keep myself out of the air. I don't know when I got cold but my head breaks the surface of the

ments. Sometimes I feel happy in the places I'm supposed to. I wonder how much they're hiding too.

Before we go, Mira says she thinks she knows someone else who'd want me to teach them piano and takes my number to pass on. I watch her and Danny chatting and wonder if they're together. Ellie hugs me when we leave. I guess she knows this game too. I say, 'See you soon.'

39

When I was a child I made houses out of Duplo. I spent hours thinking about where the fridge should go, so that my little Duplo families wouldn't be in the way of one another if someone was washing up and someone else wanted to open the fridge. Where to put the beds and the bathroom and the flowers in the gardens and which colour bricks the different rooms should be, and when I was sure that I'd made the perfect house, I'd move everyone in and spend days giving them lives, and they'd become completely real until – one day – I started to believe that maybe I was a little Duplo person and God was just someone playing with her toys like me, and that we weren't real but were dolls or something, just in someone's head; and then I found myself completely amazed at the size of that person's imagination that they could hold the stories of so many of us as well as our toys, in so many countries.

Then it'd be time to put the Duplo family away and I'd actually sob at this point because I felt like I was killing my little Duplo people and I was so worried that one day the girl in heaven who was playing with us would stop wanting to, and then the world would end. And that idea was so painful for me that I'd draw pictures of the trees and close my eyes and pretend to be sitting on a cliff or be a bird or something, and I'd always calm down again. This was just when I was a child, so I think with that level of worry over Duplo, I was always going to find sad things overwhelming.

40

There's a roof terrace on the top of Frank's house where I go on Thursday nights. That's when he hosts the drawing class downstairs so I know I'll always find him there, and I sit in the sky and wait for him. Frank's building is buried into the streets that climb up from the shore so there's only a slip of the coast in view, but you can feel the salt in the air and hear the seagulls and the waves.

I sit wrapped up in a blanket reading John Ashbery, or listening to the news, or practising the French grammar I'm trying to re-teach myself from school. When everyone's left he comes up to join me and tells me stories: about magic tricks where he'd make Ian fly over the crowd, or the little nifty ones that were his favourites, like conjuring ice into a drink or turning scrambled eggs fried. He always catches me unaware with a little flourish of magic mid-story; tonight he pulls candles out of the air as it gets dark and blows on them to light them.

It's cold, and he's brought me up an extra pair of socks from a huge bag he keeps on a hook by the ladder that leads up and outside, and a box-baked camembert, and we sit huddled by a big heater, pushing through the cold until our bodies get warm and sleepy in the way that makes your mind wander to ideas you wouldn't think of if you were inside or it was daytime.

We're sitting up there in deckchairs and he points out the stars. He tells me to come here whenever I feel full of holes, because from this far away the stars look even smaller than it's possible for a person to feel.

He knows all the names of the constellations but not which is which, and sometimes he makes the names up anyway. Tonight he tells me I should take this approach to my life: point at it and give it a name. He says, 'What matters is making a decision. Now tonight the important decision is mulled cider or ginger tea. But don't worry, because whatever you choose, we can always have the other one later on.'

I choose the ginger and stir in a spoonful of honey.

'Ah, we need a fork for the camembert,' Frank says. 'Keep stirring for a bit, Holly. A little longer. And stop.'

I pull the spoon out from the tea and it's turned into a fork. 'How did you do that?'

I don't want to get sentimental about Frank, Sam, because he does have really bad road rage and a tendency to drink too much and fall asleep in the middle of an argument when he knows he isn't making any sense, and actually he is really bad at drawing, and he and I quite often disagree about books, and in many ways Frank is just another Frank. But he really knows how to listen and to answer and he just laughs the whole time and really cares about people and tells really good stories that go with red wine and cheese. He does magic too, and these days I need to have something to believe in.

Frank asks me if I believe in God. I say I'm not too sure and we speak about how he's a Jew and a little bit about my Duplo idea, although I don't think that at all anymore and we laugh about it but we're a bit sad too, maybe because the world does sometimes feel like it's going to end. We talk about you; I've told them now, and he gives me another blanket and a piece of cake.

We sit quietly for a while, and around 10 p.m. Danny arrives. He's come straight from work and brings a newspaper he's picked up in the Co-op. Sometimes Ellie comes too; sometimes it's just me and Frank. I slot into his evening along grooves that feel much older than just a few months. I say, 'You shouldn't work so late, Danny DeVito. You've missed the sunset.'

'I always miss the sunset,' Danny replies.

'Well exactly!' says Frank. 'Have a beer.'

Frank reads us the headlines. Perched on the top of a building it feels like we could see the other side of the world if we tried hard enough. We talk about whether it's possible for peace to exist anywhere. The paper is full of the Middle East and revolution in Egypt. Firing has intensified rapidly in Gaza, and Frank's face is sad in a way I rarely see on him.

'I spent a year in Israel; I went to practise my Hebrew,' Frank says. He puts the paper down and stands up. He walks to the edge of the roof and looks out over the town.

'My family survived the Holocaust, and now there's me – Jewish and gay – a double whammy. But my life is filled with all this joy. What can I do with all that, of surviving, when a generation later there's another people, another family being jerked apart by power and bloodlines. It makes me so angry.'

He turns back to us.

'Peace isn't as effective as bloodshed,' Danny says. 'You know that, Frank. Real revolution means we all have to kill or die and that it isn't a choice of ideology but of survival.'

'What's that got to do with it?' Frank says. 'It's easy for you to say things like that when you're sat here safe with a beer in your hand, Danny. It would seem less impressive to be a radical if you had a gun in your face or soldiers attacking girls on your street.'

I read a lot of stuff I get from Danny: articles and commentaries and poems. I sit in the Jubilee Library, or in the internet cafe up by the station, and read the emails he sends me with bits of stuff in. I send him things back. We disagree a lot of the time but I find it interesting. Sometimes the things he says remind me of you. Now he's shaking his head at Frank.

'The West is too embroiled in the power games and armament of so-called terrorists for me not to already be complicit in that. I'm not trying to be a radical but to acknowledge my part in what's happening. Sometimes we have to challenge our own complacency.'

I don't know if this is something you would say. I don't feel complacent but my toes are cold.

41

We celebrate our second anniversary on the balcony of your new flat. You've paid the deposit with the advance from your new job and you haven't got furniture yet, or had time to unpack. We kiss on the bare mattress you've put on the floor.

Your mum calls while we wait for a takeaway to arrive and we put her on speakerphone.

'*Ta propre maison: ça m'a rendu très fière.* And how is your music, Holly Moon? Have you written me that song yet? *Sam, dites-lui. Tu as ta propre maison; je voudrais ma propre chanson.*'

I laugh.

'It's written. Has Sam not played it to you yet? I'll give it to him next time he comes home.'

'*Quoi! Ce n'est pas juste.* You've never written a song for me.'

Your sister chimes in, 'Come home with him, Holly. You can sing it to Mum yourself.'

We say goodnight.

'*Bisous. Fais de beaux rêves.*'

The food arrives and we sit outside to eat it with plastic cutlery straight from the silver-foil containers. We have noodles and crispy beef and chicken in black-bean sauce and we eat slowly. I love this game we play, eating in tiny bites, swallowing, stretching out the time until we take off our clothes on your bed. It surprises me sometimes, that even after this long we still take mouthfuls of each other so urgently.

That night you tell me this is the beginning of the future. You own a little piece of the city now, and one day you want to own it with me. You tell me you want to have children: twins, a girl and a boy. If not here then in another house: a family we can watch fly. I laugh at you.

'Not now,' you say. 'I know not now. But we have forever to dream about, don't we? I love this forever with you. You are so beautiful, little kite.'

42

Later, I walk halfway home with Danny. I ask him about work.

'What kind of music do you do the artwork for?'

'It's a mixture,' he says. 'I mostly work on garage and grime. But lots of different stuff really. You're a singer, aren't you? I found some of your stuff online.'

'You googled me? Danny that is stalker activity.'

'I liked it; you have a great voice. And I google everyone so don't be flattered.'

'You're an indiscriminate stalker, sure, like that makes it better.'

We laugh.

'How are you doing, Holly?' he says. 'Stuff must be tough.'

I don't know the answer to this, so I smile, and shrug, and offer him a mint.

43

Every time I think about the future I feel like I'm inside out, and my skin gets clammy. I know I can't run away to the sea to live in a rented room with a single bed and a kettle forever. But I don't know what I'm doing with my life, and it feels like all the things I knew for sure are falling away.

There are moments where I sit on the floor between my bed and the wall where I've scratched the paper away, and I can feel a hole pushing through me from the carpet to the ceiling, like I've lost this dream and lost all this stuffing that the dream had filled me with, and I've lost you too.

And that's the bit that makes me feel as though the hole going through me doesn't exist, because I don't even feel like I have a body anymore. I sit here on the floor of my room below the window and the view of the sky and feel like I am nothing.

44

It's Noel's turn to host the book club and we do it at the end of October. Noel has seven shirts that are exactly the same and he wears one of them every day. He lives in a little flat with his partner Joan, who cooks for us but doesn't stay for the discussions. I've slipped outside onto the patio for a cigarette halfway through the conversation and meet her there, smoking too. She nods as I light up and says, 'You ever been fishing?'

I tell her I haven't and she says that she and Noel go at the weekend sometimes. She says to let them know if I fancy it, that it's a nice way to pass the day: smoking and fishing. I thank her, say that'd be nice and go back in to finish talking about *Moby Dick*. I'm playing that game again, the one where I smile and move my hands to show I'm having a good time.

Frank sits next to me, muttering a commentary in my ear. He watches as the argument gets more and more heated and only joins in when it reaches the height of controversy, pushing Noel and Gabriella's disagreement over the edge.

She and I wash up together in the kitchen afterwards.

'When are you coming over to learn how to cook?' she asks. 'Sundays. Any Sunday. Come every week if you want.'

I haven't seen Gabriella since the first book club. I look at her and she smiles, and I wonder if she's known about you all along, or if Frank did anyway, and he told her.

'OK,' I say. 'Thanks. That sounds good.'

We leave together, planning recipes for the weekend. She offers Frank a lift home, but he shakes his head.

'I need the walk to calm me down. These nights get me very excited.'

I watch him pace down the street away from us with Harris, and think about how he found me at exactly the moment I needed him to.

45

Autumn has sapped the trees of their chlorophyll and stained them with dying colours: beautiful bruising as they fade away. It's Halloween next week and we're making buckwheat pancakes with caramelised onions and goats cheese and a rich beetroot soup in Gabriella's kitchen. At first, I sit on the surface of her kitchen worktop and watch her cook. She starts to give me tasks, and soon I'm helping her with cutting and peeling.

I'm in charge of making sure the soup doesn't burn, tasting it for flavour. I sing along quietly to her radio and she dances as she chops. When we sit and eat together she tells me stories about Joseph and I talk about you. It's like uncorking a bottle of champagne. Neither of us can stop; memories trickle out in bubbles and we talk until it's been dark for hours. She drives me home with a Tupperware full of soup in my lap.

46

On Bonfire Night we watch the fireworks from Frank's roof. Noel heats up jacket potatoes on a little gas stove we've taken up there and hands them round in silver foil. Jackie's brought the leftover cake from her cafe and we eat it after the potatoes, pushing sweet sticky lumps of brownie into our mouths. Frank's wired a little CD player up, and Frank Sinatra bellows out over the rooftops until the night takes over and fireworks start shooting round us in all directions. I stand there and think about you. Last year we spent Bonfire Night at different parties and at exactly the same time we texted each other: *I love you.* I remember thinking it was because the same sky was stretched over both of us. Tonight I want to peel it away and fall off the earth. I get my phone out to text you again but I don't know what I'd say.

I think about the way I used to feel you breathing when you held me, my cheek against your ribcage. I think about your fingers in my hair and the way you'd always stand next to me to clean your teeth, watching me clean mine in the mirror. I think about waking up in the morning to your open mouth and the space between your thighs where I'd hook my leg, and then I can't think about it anymore, and I turn back to today, and I slowly eat another jacket potato.

Frank comes and stands next to me, and puts an arm around my shoulders.

'I'm feeling a bit overwhelmed,' I say.

'Yeah, I know,' he replies. 'But the thing to remember about fireworks is they're just colourful farts that someone's set fire to.'

He flicks his hand at the sky and a rocket explodes, settling in the shape of a heart before disappearing.

'It won't always be this hard.'

47

Last autumn, I didn't take the bins out enough and you were always home late and it was stuffy in the flat with the heating on and too cold without it. I'd be asleep when you got home in the week, and I was mad at you, but now I missed you and that made me even angrier.

48

I hug Frank, and we shuffle closer to the others but I'm still somewhere else. Noel's telling a story about going skinny dipping as a teenager. He and his friends had made a bonfire, and chucked their clothes down next to it as they'd run into the sea. When they got back he realised he'd thrown his straight into it. He'd had to walk back home stark naked and endure weeks of being called Burnt Nuts Noel.

I laugh again because everyone else is laughing too. I think about what we all look like from the sky, tiny people making noises no one hears. Ellie slips round next to me and fills up my glass. She smiles and says, 'Come and stay at mine tonight. There's something lurking in your eyes that makes me think you should be tucked up with Auntie Ellie and not on your own in that cramped room.'

I thank her and nod but then I feel selfish and ask, 'Are you OK?'

She shrugs, 'I'm a bit hungry.'

She laughs and takes my hand and we're walking back to her house before I have time to reply.

49

We go to the pub for lunch one November Sunday and you push some swede around your plate. There is nothing to say. I try to make a few jokes but they aren't funny. We look out of the window for a bit.

I want to tell you I feel lonely. I love you just as much as ever but I am bitter about the fact you don't say thank you when I make you packed lunches and only seem to notice me when my hairs clog the bath.

On the way home from the pub you take a phone call from work, so we walk along the river while you talk to them and I play with the hole on the middle finger of my right glove.

We walk all the way back, you on the phone, me getting more and more wound up, having conversations in my head about how I never see you anymore, and the one time we have gone out you're working again.

When we get back to the house you go straight into the living room – still on the phone – and close the door. I stand there for a moment, unsure where to go. Our bedroom has clothes on the floor and anyway, I don't want to be on the bed, so I go into the kitchen. We've left some breakfast things out. I clear them away and start to clean. Half an hour later I've drunk two cups of tea and washed all the surfaces twice, and I'm pissed off.

When I go into the living room, you're sat there watching TV.

'You're done with your call?'

'Er, yeah.'

'Didn't you think you could have come and told me? I've been on my own cleaning the kitchen!'

'I don't know. I just assumed you were busy. Holly, what's wrong?'

'Are you being serious? You close the door on me, don't talk to me and then just leave me in the kitchen cleaning up after you while you're in here watching *Come Dine with Me*!'

'It's not *Come Dine with Me*. It's *MasterChef*.'

'It's the same thing!'

'No it's not.'

'It is!'

'Seriously it's not; it's a whole different format –'

'Are you joking?'

I can't understand how you don't get what I'm saying. I've just washed up your porridge bowl because you were using the sofa as your office, you haven't talked to me for fifty minutes, and it turns out you're just sitting here watching people chop up a fucking onion. I storm out of the room and slam the door.

50

My Sundays with Gabriella become something of a ritual. Frank's been teaching me to bake cakes too, so sometimes I practise while she cooks dinner. If it's a Sunday evening – rather than an afternoon – she puts on a film while we cook. Afterwards, I walk home clutching little parcels of food for the week ahead: soups and spicy chicken and these deep-fried goats cheese and beetroot balls. They're my favourite; they fall apart in my mouth, sticky cheese infecting the earthiness of the beetroot with an oozing sweetness, coated in breadcrumbs, the creamy molten flavour dissolving on my tongue.

They're the best thing I've ever tasted. Gabriella teaches me to cook them for my dad's birthday, but the weekend I'm due to go home I change my mind. I don't know what I'd do with myself there, in the warmth of my parents' sitting room. Instead I send a text to wish him happy birthday and I drift here, to the shore.

There's a fog in my head, matched by the wet haze clogging up the sky and making everywhere an effort to get to. I feel cold. I imagine picking up my phone and calling someone: Ellie or Gabriella or my parents or Frank. I know my mouth won't co-operate though; my tongue is too thick between my teeth and my face won't move.

51

For our November meeting we're at Jackie's house and we read *The Collector*. Noel tells us he's a lepidopterist too; he has his own collection of moths and butterflies at home. He says he's surprised by the way the book links collecting butterflies with imprisonment. He tells us that when butterflies die they become brittle and locked into a kind of rigor mortis that snaps their wings closed. The process used to collect them is called relaxing, and helps them unfold again. He says he's always thought of this softening as a release, and that – in truth – in order to collect butterflies you have to understand how to set them free not how to keep them locked up.

'But setting things free can be painful too,' Frank says. I'm too tired to work out what he means.

52

You feel so real still that whenever my phone rings I look down and expect to see your name. I leave you a voicemail and feel ashamed. I'm starting to miss you in a new way that feels like I'm being ripped up into little pieces and hurled hard in your direction, only for the wind to pick up all the bits of me and fling them the opposite way.

53

I go to meet Ellie from the library where she's studying. I've made fridge cake and it's been semi-successful so I take her a piece wrapped in cling film. When I get home that night I pull it out of my bag and put it on the side: unoffered. I feel angry with myself; I see Ellie all the time and couldn't exactly have failed to notice the gaps in her body or the fact that if I go for food with Sean or Danny she arrives after we've eaten. But I say nothing and pretend not to notice.

As my baking gets better I gain confidence, and with confidence I gain flair. Under Frank's exuberant coaching and Gabriella's expertise I mix beetroot and chocolate or apple and rum, and one day Frank decides that one of my cakes should go to Jackie's cafe with his to be sold. I offer to go on the cake run before work the following morning. I often go anyway, popping in to say hi to Jackie on my way to my first house of the day. She always gives me a coffee she won't let me pay for, so I put a pound in the tip box and slip away to drink it in the street as I weave through commuters and ironed shirts, and silently guess the names of the people I pass in my head: *Becky, Aidan, Jennifer, Jay, Edith.*

That morning – armed with the cakes we've baked – I arrive ten minutes early and sit inside with my coffee, smiling as I watch what we've made get sold to the breakfast crowd; Jackie's wink as she hands it over makes me want to climb onto the table and jump off again cheering.

On the counter by the till Jackie keeps a huge glass sweet jar with little slips of paper in it, each of them with a word and its meaning neatly typed across it. I stick my hand in as I put my coffee cup back on the counter and say goodbye, and as I swing the door shut behind me and step out into the swell of people whisking themselves off to their mornings, I look down and read: *'Sonder, noun: the realisation that each random passerby is living a life as vivid and complex as your own.'*

54

What I want to know, Sam, is will I ever run out of things I wish I could tell you? Things that sit in my fingerprints you'll never get to read there. What about the things you know would make me laugh? Are they really just gone now?

55

At the following week's pub quiz we come second. We celebrate with red wine, generously poured and drunk too fast. I've come straight to the pub from work without eating and the alcohol is quickly starting to flow in my blood. I start to feel my fingertips buzzing as I get tipsier.

The noise in the pub is heightened, and the temperature of the room is warmer because the outside is so cold. We're in the corner: Ellie and I, sparring with Duane about something. Sean is listening – amused – his fingers drumming on the table to the song that's playing through the speaker system. Mira is at the bar picking up another round and Danny's gone to help her, me just conscious of my inclination to watch them together. I'm still unsure if they're more than friends and I'm even less sure why it would matter to me either way.

Danny sits down next to me when they come back, and when I say I'm cold he puts his arm round me. I let him, but it doesn't warm me up.

56

It's 4 a.m. and I've been in love with you for almost five years. We're lost in Soho on our way home from a party and we can't find a taxi. There's a sweaty woman in a doorway dressed in navy blue. It's been raining and the pavement shines like her armpits. Someone walking past says, 'We won't be allowed in there again.' The ground tips; my toes are numb. There's a bouquet of flowers in the road. Its cellophane dances in the wind. I tell you I'm jealous of the rain on your face. You laugh into my mouth and I have never felt so happy.

My stomach hurts, partly from the wine, swinging like a magnet in the roundness above my hips. Partly from the laughing. We push our mouths together again. Waterlogged and clumsy. The sweaty woman's gone. We find another street to swing down.

57

I teach four children the piano now. I like watching their hands move over the keys. Sometimes I open up the lid and get them to watch the little hammers at work while I play. I tell them it's good to understand why the sound comes out like it does, and they watch it like it's magic.

Sometimes Frank walks down to the sea with me and throws stone after stone into the water, like he's playing a piano. He makes the splashes get bigger and bigger until the water dances in rhythm. I know it's fine not to understand why it moves like it does, and I watch it because it's magic.

58

In the last week of November we finally win the quiz and we go dancing afterwards to celebrate. The music is louder than I'm expecting and the bodies and the noise around me make me dizzy. I feel battered by the beat of the bass and I don't know how much longer I can keep standing. I'm worried I'll get trampled. Someone's dancing right behind me now with their back rubbing against mine and I don't want them to touch me. Someone else pushes into me as they jostle past. All these feet stomping to the music.

I look around; Mira is with Duane and Danny a little way away and I can't see Ellie and Sean; I think maybe they're smoking outside. I can't remember how to breathe. I'm hot, so I try to get to the exit but there are too many people in here. They're twisting their bodies into rectangles and boxes and shapes that bodies shouldn't be in. A tingling starts in my fingers and I'm starting to get black dots in my eyes and suddenly your arms are round me; you're holding me up and I start to cry, shaking all the panic out into your shoulder, but it's a small hand that wiggles into mine and when you step away to look at me you're not you; you're Sean, and it's Ellie saying, 'It's OK, Holly.' And I tell her, 'He's dead, Ellie; he's dead.'

about visiting a friend there but headed instead to Covent Garden, and then down past Piccadilly to Regent Street.

It was busy – I mean of course it was – it was a summer evening in the West End so the streets and shops were heaving: steaming with the heat of tourists and vendors and the rats under the ground. I had quite a heavy bag from where I'd been staying at your house and I was sweating and needed the loo. I kept thinking about this Denise Riley poem that you would've felt apathetic towards – and I say apathetic because you wouldn't have understood it, but you wouldn't have minded that you didn't understand – not like me who would've really hated something because of that – but you, you would have just read it and felt nothing or only very mild consternation, and thinking about that was making me really angry because I'd made an effort with economics for fuck's sake, and we'd hardly ever talked about reading, and all the books you owned were two copies of *Jude the Obscure*, and I'd never understood why you needed two copies, especially in comparison to your lack of other things; I mean you didn't own any pens on the principle that you typed everything, and after you lost your phone charger you didn't bother to buy a new one and always just used mine and you had no mugs or a corkscrew and no soap – ever – but you did have two copies of *Jude the Obscure*. And when I asked you about it, you didn't tell me it was because you loved it, and loved Hardy, and had bought both copies because it was the best thing you'd ever read; you just said nothing, didn't even acknowledge it actually, and I felt like that would have been your reaction had I shown you this poem that the line I had stuck in my head had come from. And maybe I'm not being fair but I was feeling sort of sweaty from the bag and the sun and the buses and my make-up, which was running off a bit – and that was the Riley line, about *how much mascara washes away each day and internationally* – and I didn't feel angry, not really, except in my knuckles, which were getting clenchy, and the back of my neck where I felt a bit sick, and I wasn't angry but I did feel like I might burst into tears at any moment and I just wanted – needed even – to be absolutely still.

So I stood in the street and I cried, and it came out really loudly so I faced a shop wall. I didn't want anyone to think they had to talk to me. I stood and sobbed loudly and kicked the wall and shouted at it, 'Fuck,' mostly. 'Fuck, fuck, fuck.'

Then it started to hurt, so I started walking again, up Oxford Street and right onto James Street and up onto Marylebone High until I reached this bar that looked alright, and I went in and used the loo and the mirror and ordered a glass of wine that I couldn't really afford, and sat down at a table facing away from the window, with my back touching it almost; my back was directly against the window. And I didn't look around; I just looked straight ahead mostly, and I felt like I was making a tunnel spanning out from my head that bore into everything around me: the light bulbs, people, walls, ceiling. And I filled the tunnel with white noise and I sat perfectly still. I could still feel the city moving around me – because of the tunnel it felt like a long way away, but this actually seemed to make it move faster – and it seemed to be moving like wheels: spinning with the bicycles and cars and men on unicycles in Covent Garden and the balls they're always juggling. The spinning was spinning too, and suddenly someone was telling me that the table I was sitting at was reserved for someone else, and I looked around and all the other tables were full, so I stood by the bar: sipping my wine until it was empty and eating a bowl of pasta, slowly, standing there amongst all the people jostling for drinks and tequila shots and little pots of olives and then drinks again.

And all this time everyone else was spinning around me, like the people were turning cartwheels and the bar staff were clowns or tap dancers, and their feet were shuffling and stamping, and the people in the bar were shouting and the shouting just got louder as more of them shouted, and the music – although it didn't have a heavy bass or anything – was still louder than just an itch or an irritation, and it honestly felt like the music and the shouting was hitting me over the head, or in my head, even: hitting me on my brain. And the noise got louder and all up in my armpits which were sweating again and I was still standing there, like a silent drill or something, and I felt really frightened, like I wanted to scream – actually scream – from my intestines or my stomach or wherever a scream comes from: my hips maybe. I couldn't scream though, like I couldn't cry anymore, like I couldn't finish my pasta because my mouth was suddenly dry, and what I really wanted at that exact moment was not to be there with all those wheels and the circus and the spinning and the city with its gutters full of banana peel and copies of *Metro* and dust blowing in circles around me.

3

Now I'm by the sea and it's winter. This year the excitement of advent – roast nuts and ice skating and wrapping paper – feels a long way away. The sky is stripes of grey and white and steel blue. I bury myself in cleaning jobs, take on extra work and stop answering my phone. I don't want to hear people being kind. I'm going back to London and I feel like I'm going to see you and I know I won't, but I don't know what to do about that.

I keep walking past the mini Christmas market outside the shopping centre and thinking about last year when we went to Winter Wonderland and drank mulled wine on a picnic table by that ridiculous talking Rudolph. And when my hands get cold I think about you being there to hold them.

I buy you a present and wrap it up and write a little card that says: *I miss you. Merry Christmas.* I post it to your mum's house in York, and after it slips out of my hand into the mouth of the letter box I go for a run, slapping my feet down on the dry, frozen concrete and filling my lungs with air that scratches my throat and tugs at my face with the cold. I run for an hour, listening to Christmas carols on my iPod and letting my muscles find a frantic, whirling rhythm that's just too fast to be comfortable.

I run past Jackie's cafe on the way home but don't look in through the window. When I get back I turn the shower up a bit too hot and feel the water dig into my muscles. My skin is burnt when I get out and I can't sleep so I sit outside again and watch the sea. It's angry, like it doesn't want to be part of the ground when it's the colour of the sky. By the time I go back to bed there's a thickness in my chest and my throat is sore.

4

After you died I tried to smell you everywhere. I stayed at your mum's house in York for the funeral and no one was sleeping in the room she'd decided was yours. It stood like an empty bottle of red wine in the recycling, stained by you.

I stood in there after the service: wanting to be on my own, or with you, or both. Your coat was still hanging on the back of the door. I remember thinking you must have been cold in the ambulance.

I took it off the hook and put it on. I put my right hand into your pocket and pulled out some spearmint chewing gum and three paper clips you'd threaded together.

You told me once that I love the smell of sun cream because the parts of our brain that smell things are in the same bit that memory is. You told me smell and memory are built the same way, and so sun cream makes me think of holidays.

I sat there, crying on your bed. I pushed my nose into your sleeve and inhaled, but you'd gone.

5

Frank decides he's going to take me on what he calls a Chrismukkah trip to London to visit Borough Market. I think he knows I'm dreading going back and wants to give me a practice run. We do it on the second weekend in December – as Hanukkah begins – and we take a fast train to Victoria. There's a woman there in a Santa hat with a four-piece band, singing carols with lots of vibrato and jangling a bucket with a cancer charity logo on the side. People are already milling furiously: bags crammed into clenched, sweaty fists and armpits stuffed with parcels. Hands flick at ticket gates and hips swing through them to plunge towards escalators: down the steps, turn left, up the stairs, swipe at the barrier, swing to the left and eastbound, more stairs, platform. Doors open and beep and close and speed under the ground, slicing through the networks of bars and shops and mosques and traffic lights and dustbins. It all gets up inside me and I don't know which bits to feel.

We take the District line as far as Embankment and cross Hungerford Bridge. We dip down onto the Southbank and walk along past the Queen Elizabeth Hall and the National, on towards the market. Frank smiles at me as we emerge into the daylight and our feet slap the concrete path of the river bank.

The cold air gets inside my chest and makes me cough, so we walk slowly. I'm scared by the familiarity of the noises, and the river, and the fairy lights in the trees. It's what I've been running from. At the skate park the rush of wheels and the smack down of a board jerking onto the ground merges with the voices of more buskers: a choir twirling 'Jingle Bells' out in robust harmony. It's caught by the wind and by the feet of children who've broken away from their parents to dance in front of it: tiny arms bent and feet kicking with startling, ridiculous joy. We stop to watch for a bit and Frank sings along.

At Borough Market we're surrounded by people – almost so many we can't move – and they work like an anaesthetic; I can't think about anything else. We drink mulled wine and eat turkey rolls, mine loaded up with bacon too: the hot salty meat collapsing on our tongues with each mouthful and oozing its juices. I'm talking quickly, pointing things out to Frank like a flag clutching at wind: flapping in its gusts and scared of being still. We laugh at everything: the tourists' excitement and the over-zealous enthusiasm of little children. We're caught up in it. We eat sweet tarts that fall off our forks and are shovelled in with hands instead, etching their hot liquids into our fingerprints and steam scalding our tongues. Frank buys a huge cheese for our last book club of the year; I tell him it's the size of a head, so he calls it Percy. We suck in the smells of wood and pepper, and thick hot fats that glimmer alongside sweating dough and crisp, sharp vegetables.

6

Sitting on a bed you'd slept in twice, I listen to your relatives downstairs sharing hot, sweet drinks and sangah and brochette. They speak in French and Yemba and I can't remember who lots of them are. I feel so far away from you.

You gave me a lift to a rehearsal once, for a gig I was doing in Guildford. I didn't know exactly where the venue was and we drove down the same road three times while I tried to get to grips with the map. You were furious, unable to understand how I could find it so hard to navigate. You pulled over to look at the map yourself and I sang John Denver's 'I'm Sorry' at you, changing the lyrics to make it about driving and Guildford and me being useless, until you laughed and threw the map at my head.

You told me, 'You're intolerable,' and kissed me.

I sit there, smelling for you in the arm of your coat, and looking at the tiny pink roses on the wallpaper. You would've hated them. I think it's odd in a newly built house, which are normally very neutral, and I wonder what would happen if I need to go to Guildford again.

Your sister Danielle slips upstairs with a plate of food for me and we lie on the bed together.

'You know,' she says. 'One of my uncles just told me there's a Yemba proverb where if you scratch the skull of someone who's died, you can save them.'

She looks at me. Her eyes are a bit watery, but she's smiling ironically.

'Shall we dig him up?' I say.

We both start laughing. It isn't funny at all but it's a relief to feel something. After a while your mum comes up carrying Alfie and says, 'He was looking for you.'

Danielle takes him and we all stand there looking at each other – tired and numb – your mum and your sister and your nephew and me.

7

When we've exhausted the market we walk back out into the refracted light of the waterside and keep going east, ducking under the criss-cross of balconies at Shad Thames and stopping by the Design Museum to sit and drink coffee.

I'm startled by the calm but Frank fills the quiet with conversation. He tells me about the day he met Ian. He was working in Covent Garden at the time, and most days Ian would come to watch his show. Frank would watch him watching him but he'd always disappear into the crowds as soon as Frank finished. Frank tells me he'd been trying to pluck up the courage to say hello, and then one morning he'd been cycling into work and a cat had run out in the road. Swerving to avoid it, he'd veered onto the pavement and driven straight into Ian. Ian had let Frank buy him a coffee to say sorry, and the two had barely spent a moment apart since.

'You have to understand, it was illegal then,' Frank said. 'We had to be so careful, but we knew we wanted to be together.'

They'd practised magic and travelled the country, and then the world, performing, and they'd settled in Brighton when arthritis had slowed Ian's knees and they'd wanted to live a bit more quietly.

There's a baby in a pram just along from where we're sitting, and while Frank is talking I watch it play with a plastic hoop that rattles when it's shaken. The baby laughs every time it hears the noise, and its parents laugh at it laughing. It makes me feel sad.

Maybe Frank's been watching the baby too because now he's saying how he and Ian didn't really think about children; even when things had got easier they were so used to being just them. They'd grown friends instead, he says.

'We felt like there were people who loved us as much as children would've done. There are certainly enough people in my life I love. There are no lingering regrets.'

He smiles, and looks away over the river, but I can see he's crying.

'I miss him every day,' he says.

Frank and I pay for the coffees and walk back to the tube. Frank's sad. I wish I could do magic to make it better, but that's what he does. Instead, I hold his arm and we drift.

We look around at Christmas disguising the city's aches in bright lights and music. We smile and laugh at things and let life look the way we want it to feel. I wonder if lonely people just need to be around other lonely people sometimes.

I want the day to seep out of me in dreams that rattle like the underground, and smell of cloves, and pork, and river salt. But even in sleep I'm panicked, like there's something I've forgotten to do, someone I've forgotten how to be.

8

We have a week of cold blue skies. The starlings swirl over the old pier. They shake in the sky: tiny wings moving fast to keep them up. I don't know where they're going. They don't seem to want to leave. We watch each other moving, travelling nowhere. The sea curls, throws itself at the rocks. I go for long runs. My muscles shake and I try to be still.

9

It's Sunday and we're making a Christmas roast. Gabriella tells me this is the hardest time of year for her. She says the first year after Joseph died she'd told all her friends she wanted to spend the day alone. On Christmas Eve she'd chopped all the vegetables, stuffed the turkey and put a Christmas cake in the oven. She says she felt giddy, hysterical with excitement almost, her body numb and anaesthetised by the carols she played all day on her CD player. That night – before bed – she filled a stocking and put it by Joseph's pillow. She'd been shopping for him for months, buying utensils and CDs and a calendar for his wall. She'd wrapped every little present and crammed them into his Christmas sock with sweets and oranges and handfuls of nuts. On Christmas morning she'd woken up and crept into his room, ready to see him sitting there unwrapping his presents.

She tells me that on Christmas Day – when she saw his empty bed and still-bulging stocking – she'd really known he was gone. She says she hadn't even realised she was crying until her legs gave way. She'd lain on his bedroom floor, staring up at his map of the world. Then she'd climbed into his bed and cried some more and unwrapped all the presents she'd bought for him, laying them out on the bed around her. Eventually she fell asleep, tucked between clean sheets and dreaming of nothing, her mind tired by the sharp Christmas sting and the strange hole inside her where love seemed to be trying to stay alive.

Frank and Ian eventually woke Gabriella up by ringing on her door around 4 p.m. Pretending they'd forgotten it was Christmas Day, they told her they'd popped round to see if she fancied a stroll by the sea with Harris. Together they'd walked along the seafront – Gabriella and Ian hand in hand – and they'd eaten fish and chips out of paper cones on the pier. They'd done it every Christmas since, and Gabriella and Frank had kept doing it alone after Ian had died too.

She cries when she tells me this. I don't say anything. I'm tired and my head aches and I don't care about Gabriella's son, who I've never met and never will because he's dead. I leave before we've finished cooking and brush off her offer of a lift home. I know I'm not going back to my room anyway. I sit on the beach with a bottle of cough mixture and I sob.

10

Yesterday my big toe cut a hole in my tights. The nails are too long but I can't find the clippers. The open window lets in the sound of wind, and I see naked tree curls and crisp packets blowing like tiny kites across the pavement. They can't take off into the sky. My feet are chilly. When I scrunch up my toes they catch on the carpet. The ladder from where the hole is moves up my tights in a thin, waving line. There's frost in my belly. I'm not used to being cold without you; your back – broad and smooth as a playground slide – was last year's winter.

11

In December the book club meet at Ellie's. She's chosen *Life of Pi*. The film has just come out and she wants to read the book before she sees it. We meet on 13th December: eight days before I'm due to go home for Christmas. Everyone exchanges gifts and mince pies and hugs, but I can't think of anything to say, even though I read the book and I liked it. I'm aware of people talking to me and answering them but I don't know what we're saying. I'm tired, Sam, and my chest hurts. I smile a lot and we're all so happy and I think maybe I run home afterwards, but I don't remember exactly how I got there.

12

On the 16th December a physiotherapy student in Delhi goes to see the film of *Life of Pi* and on her bus journey home she's attacked. I read about it in an internet cafe the day after, before my first cleaning job of the last week before Christmas.

Three days before, twenty-six people have been shot at a US primary school: twenty of them children. That evening – the

17th – Bradley Wiggins is named BBC Sports Personality of the Year, and 16,000 Chinese lanterns are let off in Mexico in a world-record attempt.

I don't care about any of this. I have little cuts on my knuckles from where I'm scrubbing things so hard. My shoulders ache from hoovering.

On 21st December – the day that according to the Mayan Calendar the world is supposed to end – I catch the train home. My mum's eyes fill with tears when she opens the door and she tries to wipe them away so I only see her smile. I pretend too, and smile back.

'Merry Christmas!' I say.

13

Every Christmas Eve my brother and I sit at the table in our kitchen and peel potatoes. We put on Christmas socks and a CD of carols. After the potatoes are done my brother puts a layer of marzipan on the Christmas cake and I make royal icing to flick into stiff, snowy peaks all over it, topping it off with little snowmen and robins and Father Christmases.

This year we go through the motions as usual. I can't tell if I'm really there but my brother keeps squeezing my hand and sometimes we sing along for a bit to the songs.

In the evening we go up to the Albert Hall to a carol service, and I remember being here before. Afterwards, we eat pizza and drink wine on the Southbank, and even though I'm not too sure what I think about God, I go to midnight mass and close my eyes to pray. I don't know if praying ever works, but I met Frank this year, so I know that magic does. I'm a bit drunk by the time we get there. I pray for flowers to grow out of my hands and for the wind to play me music, and think that if there is a God, he shouldn't need us to tell him what it is that we need.

14

At Christmas lunch I'd just started chewing a mouthful of potato and peas when I needed to be on my own. I slipped out of the room to the toilet and sat on its cold rim. The edges of the seat cut slightly into my thighs, and I looked around me at the dark wood-effect panelling. Dad has always said there were rooms more important to redecorate than the toilet, so it's lingered like a bad hangover from the people who lived in the house before. I felt grateful for it in that moment though. The weird strips of wood-coloured plastic seemed to soak up whatever I was feeling that made me need to walk away from bad cracker jokes and wine and roast parsnips, to sit on a toilet for ten minutes when I didn't need to go, and stay there even though the hole in the seat was starting to pinch the backs of my legs.

I sat on the loo and counted in my head until my breathing calmed down. Then I flushed a handful of wet tissues down the toilet, reapplied my mascara and went back to the table for Christmas pudding.

After lunch we went for a walk on the Downs. Mum and Dad had given me a new lens for my camera so I took a few photos and we had a bit of a kickabout. It was cold, in a good way, and we came home and ate leftover turkey and roast potatoes and watched the *The Sound of Music* and drank Baileys.

I'd popped outside for a cigarette halfway through and my brother joined me.

'How you doing, Holly?'

'I love Christmas. And carols; I love carols.'

'I'll sing you one now if you want,' he says. *'Good King Wenceslas looked out, on the feast of –'*

We laugh. He pulls a parcel out of his pocket and hands it to me.

'I got you an extra present. It's nothing big, it's just –'

I smile at him and unwrap it slowly. Inside is a watch with a navy-blue leather strap.

'I hope you like it. Look, Holly, everyone says that time makes stuff better, like one day we'll wake up and be in this future where everything's great. I don't believe that. We just have to make it better ourselves. You moving to Brighton, starting again on your own; it's really brave, Hols. I'm really proud of you. But keep an eye on time moving by, OK, and if it's been more than a week just let one of us know you're alright. We've all really missed you.'

'I'm sorry, Rob.'

'Don't be, I get it. Just wear the watch, OK, and know I'm thinking of you.'

It's difficult to be reminded of how it feels to be loved. I hug him and we cry for a bit while the wind blows and I smoke another cigarette, and a robin sits and watches us from the garden fence.

That evening my mobile flashes up with a number starting 01904: York. I know it's the number I deleted in the summer, the landline of the house your mum moved into eight months ago. It's the house you went up to for the weekend to help your mum move in. It's in the road where you were hit by a car, and it's where your family will be spending Christmas. I don't answer my phone.

15

At my primary school, every winter, we played conkers. There were other obsessions that took over the playground for a while, but none of them with the same reliable annual recurrence. The weather got colder and knuckles got raw and we'd go conkering.

Mum would still collect a pile every October and leave them in our porch, so on Boxing Day I asked my brother to play. We sat on the stone steps of our patio and carefully threaded five conkers each onto a string.

You win a conker fight if your conker is still on its string when your opponent's comes off and – for every battle you win – your conker gains the points of its opponent. So if you defeat a conker that's on fifteen and you're on seven; you immediately become a twenty-two pointer. This means the original conker is key, and everyone at my school favoured a certain type. For me it was a toss-up between one that's small and hard and resilient under attack, and a larger one with a lot of power behind it but less compact force in defence.

On Boxing Day we just played. Rob won, and afterwards we sat there talking: me about the kids I taught piano to and the pub quiz team, him about his girlfriend Lucy. I hadn't realised how much I'd missed him.

The next morning a little packet arrived in the post. In it was a note from Frank that said: *With love to my little baker; put this somewhere airy and bright.*

He'd sent me a little plastic bag with some buttons in it, and I emptied it out on my bedside table where the light came in.

16

Dad took me out between Christmas and the New Year to practise my driving. We took the A23 towards Reigate and I drove us down the high street, past the bell tower where the Salvation Army were out collecting money. The Christmas lights hung over the road like giant penny sweets. Dad asked me how things were and I told him alright.

'You're driving really well,' he said.

'About time. It's been seven years.'

'Don't worry about it. I didn't pass until my fifth test. Runs in the family.'

I smiled. Something crap came on the radio and we both reached out to flip the channel. 'Problem is it's all naff Christmas songs this time of year,' Dad said. He kept scrolling until he found a station playing 'Fairytale of New York'.

'Ah, I spoke too soon! A classic.'

We reached that road between Reigate and Dorking where it's flat and wide like a runway. The song was at that part where the drums kick in for the first time and Kirsty McColl's character meets Shane MacGowan's on a cold New York Christmas Eve. I put the car into fourth gear and I thought about you, the Christmas before, dressed up as Santa with Alfie on your knee. Your mum and Danielle had laughed at you singing along out of tune but he'd put his hands over your mouth and cried until you'd stopped.

The chorus started playing on the radio and I must have hit the brakes because I was standing in the road, leaning on the door. Dad got out of the passenger seat and walked round to where I was starting to crumple, sliding down the car. I let him take my weight, resting on him as cars sped past and the song finished.

'It's OK, Holly,' he said. 'It's alright.'

17

The winter of year four, my best friend Anna backed the bigger conkers while I went for small and hard. We teamed up and fought other pairs feeling completely unbeatable. By the last week of term our conkers had a joint score of 568 and everyone wanted to fight us in a bid to take our title as champions.

Three days before the Christmas holidays James Wilson and Raymond King took us on between the school shed and the netball courts. It was a Tuesday lunchtime and it was raining and Anna's conker went first. I remember the shock of seeing it split open and explode from its string across the black playground floor. It was over. Two hits later and mine was gone too. Whatever James and Ray had soaked their conkers in had worked and they were left with a massive 892 points. Our conkers were finished, the insides of their shells soft and yellow, splattered across the hopscotch court like bits of brain. Suddenly the game seemed brutal.

After the bell rang for the end of lunch I pretended I needed the loo and told Anna I'd meet her in the classroom. Instead I snuck back round to the shed and picked up all the broken pieces of conker. I covered them in a bit of kitchen roll that Mum had used to wrap up the orange in my lunch box, and when I got home that night I put on my wellies and went out into our garden. Using my blunt fingernails I dug the earth out and watched the wet soil rub into the grazes on my knuckles. I pushed my conker-born brain pieces into their little grave and put a miniature notebook I'd got in my cracker at our school Christmas dinner the day before on top. Inside I'd written James's name surrounded by hearts on the first page. James Wilson had freckles on his nose and was excellent at the recorder, but those things would never bring back the 568-point conkers that he'd stolen from me and Anna, and my love for him was over.

I thought about that conker when you died. I thought about the doctors waiting to give you a craniotomy and wondered whether – if you'd held on long enough for them to cut you open and lift the pressure on your brain pieces – you might have made it. I thought about conkers smashing into each other and about you walking out into the road. I thought about the scar above your left eyebrow, and the first time you'd told me you loved me, and about dancing with you on a street corner at midnight, sharing headphones and standing hip to hip.

I thought about you in the ambulance and about the fact I didn't know what we'd said in our last conversation. I thought about why you hadn't been wearing your coat when it was such a cold day, and what it was that made you so distracted you hadn't stopped for the traffic. I think about those things now and I wish that burying your name in a notebook surrounded by hearts would make it all go away.

18

Just before New Year I called the 01904 number back and hung up after two rings. I went to the bathroom, looked around me at the pretend wood panelling for suggestions and threw up. I took the battery out of my phone for the rest of the day so that if anyone tried to phone me again I wouldn't need to know.

When I drew my curtains that night I looked down at Frank's little pile of buttons on my bedside table. I don't know what I'd expected to happen but they seemed so stupid sat there, so I scooped them up and chucked them out the window.

19

On New Year's Eve I went to a party with a friend from school. It was at the house of one of her friends from university, and she'd persuaded me to crash and go along with her. It was a black-tie do and involved all sorts of fancy nibbles being handed round on silver trays, and proper champagne, and beautiful tiny gold decorations hanging from the ceiling at well-placed intervals across the whole of the room in a delicate kind of a way. And everyone there was really posh with surnames like Bumley-Pompington, and I've never been at home in that sort of environment anyway, but especially on New Year when I've always got smashed and done the splits and not been able to get up again, so sit spread eagled on the floor singing along to Whitney Houston, even if the song that's playing isn't by Whitney Houston.

I spent quite a bit of the first half of the evening wondering how long it had taken to fix all the dangly things onto the ceiling. I was also concerned that the tiny pieces of Sellotape would take strips off the white paint when removed. I was a bit nervous because I could feel myself getting drunk really fast, and I also knew that I was feeling weird about you, and would probably end up crying, and as soon as we'd got there I'd known that it just really wasn't that sort of an event. So I kept drinking to try and distract myself from it all, and I ate quite a lot of canapés and stood on the edges of conversations nodding and laughing.

The music at the party was the kind of music you only ever play at New Year or if you're feeling really depressed. I've never really understood why that's the same thing, but it does mean that if you're not feeling really great at New Year the music always makes you feel bleak. So I was dancing and getting worried about crying and then I was kissing a man whose name I still don't know in a room upstairs with lots of coats in it. There was a shelf in the corner of the room with a purple soft toy dragon wearing a T-shirt that said, 'Vote Alex For Welfare' on it and I asked the boy if he was Alex. He looked confused and when I pointed at the dragon he said, 'This isn't my house.'

The kissing was good but he kept using his tongue like a sledgehammer. I pulled my dress over my head and he sucked a bit on my right nipple without taking my bra off, which was awkward so I looked at the dragon and then pulled on his hair so he stopped and came back to my face. I tried to keep my lips mostly closed but he was really persistent with his tongue, which wasn't great at first but I was starting to get turned on so it got a bit better. I could taste the vodka he'd been drinking moving between our lips and something spicy that tasted like pepperoni but there wasn't any food with pepperoni in it at the party so it probably wasn't that. I thought the purple dragon felt very at odds with the room with the dangly things in it downstairs, which had a shiny wooden floor, and the man started kissing my neck and taking his trousers off so I concentrated on that.

The faint sound of the party downstairs was somehow holding me upright and I took my bra off and closed my eyes. I felt the moving and him pushed against me and my breasts pressed between us. His arm gripped round me and he pushed my knickers to one side and let his boxers gather round his ankles like a puddle. It wasn't really working so he pushed me onto the bed to get on top, and I pulled my underwear off properly. He had a long body, spilling away between my hips like a translucent tongue. That song by Bryan Adams that was Number 1 for ages and was the theme tune for *Robin Hood* came onto the speakers in the room below us. I was looking at the ceiling now so I couldn't see the dragon anymore. I didn't know how I felt about having sex in front of it so I closed my eyes. The man was sucking on my nipple again but it was the left one this time. He pushed my legs up, crab-like, and started grunting. I grunted a bit too, to remind me I was still there. I knew he was finished when his body slapped down and he lay on top of me: beached on my belly. I felt sticky. He handed me my pants and grinned. I think I smiled back and he said, 'I love this song.' I said, 'Yeah.'

He went to go to the toilet and I went downstairs. I found my friend again and sat outside on the pavement with her, crying a

or the lobsters or something. The wings went next: ripped from pigeon shoulders, and then we sliced them open, straight down the sternum to peel back the skin and expose their insides.

I don't know whether birds maybe don't have that much blood, but there was a strange, clean precision to cutting up the pigeons. My fingers and knife plied open their bodies and as bits of bird got threaded under my nails and into my pores I was struck by the intricacy of the insides I was delving into. The birds were filled with these tiny mechanisms that had kept them alive and I remember feeling something very strong about the fact they all had hearts – I mean, obviously they did; I'd always known pigeons must have hearts so it wasn't surprise I was feeling exactly – but I'd never really thought about how weird it was, and these organs looked exactly like the ones we'd learnt about in biology. I don't know whether pigeon and human hearts are the same, but it looked to me like this bird had all the atriums and ventricles and veins and capillaries leading inwards and outwards to keep its tiny body alive that we did and – maybe because I've never seen the inside of a body before – I was struck by how much more beautiful this pigeon seemed now I was looking at it inside out. It felt incredibly cruel to be cutting into something so perfect. I wondered whether – if I could turn myself inside out – my body would seem perfect too.

Years after that trip on the boat I learnt that pigeons have a very wide visual field and so – while most humans see only 180 degrees around them – pigeons can take in 340. Oddly, one of the other animals with a visual field of 340 degrees is the rat.

You liked facts like these. You would tell me that my body is beautiful, that I am a bird who should be less afraid of the sky. You would kiss the space between my legs and call me little kite and use your hands to scratch wings into my shoulder blades. I don't know if I will ever be able to let anyone love me like that again.

21

I headed back to my mum and dad's on New Year's Day with the worst hangover of my life. I had to go back to Brighton the next day to start some post-Christmas holiday cleaning but I needed to stop crying first. I don't know why I did it, but I looked at my phone to check the time and I ended up calling your mum.

She said she was pleased to hear from me and asked me how I was. I told her I'd had a bit of a chest infection before I'd come home but it seemed to be clearing up now, although I didn't think the hangover was going to help. I told her the pigeon fact and asked what she'd got for Christmas and laughed a lot, and then I started crying and we both went quiet.

I could hear her breathing into the phone and I wanted to tell her that she sounded like the sea. That I loved her son so much I thought all my bones were going to break, that I hadn't called before because there was nothing at all I could say that would change anything. The waves had taught me that, when I watched them breaking into the beach at night; even the most beautiful things are relentlessly cruel. You were the most beautiful thing.

Instead I tell her I'm sorry and that I have to go, and I hang up the phone. Afterwards I feel like screaming but my head aches and I smell of alcohol so I have a shower and go to find my parents so I don't have to be alone.

22

I drive myself back to Brighton in Mum's car, with her in the passenger seat, going the long way round to avoid the motorways. There are dead animals splattered periodically along the road and they make me flinch. *They're pigeons, not people, pigeons not people*, I think, but it doesn't work because pigeons have lungs and things too and even conkers look like they're bleeding when they're broken open on Tarmac.

When we arrive we go for a walk along the front before Mum drives home, and we sit together at the little cafe at Ovingdean, sipping coffee. I've started to play a game with hot things, holding them in my mouth for as long as I can take the burn. Mum sips hers slowly, blowing on it.

The seagulls soar over us yelping at the wind, and I wonder if they can feel the turn of the year too. I wonder if they notice winter's rotting, if they know calendars have been chucked out and gym membership rates have soared, and another January has arrived to host our circuits of hormones, rhythms, songs stuck in our heads, voices stuck in our throats, lovers stuck in our bones, and the tide crashing in again and out again like it can't find the place it wants to stay.

I wonder if the birds can hear us when we wish each other happy new year. I think they probably don't but wonder if they have taste buds in their beaks, and I ask my mum what she thinks.

She says she reckons they do but that they probably can't smell because they don't seem to have noses. I've never thought of that.

That night on the radio I listen to the news. It tells me the United Nations have released a statement saying the number of deaths in the civil war in Syria has reached 60,000, and I fall asleep dreaming of fish and chips that turn into seagulls and fall from the sky like bombs.

23

I go over to Frank's the next evening and we sit in his kitchen drinking tea.

'Harris missed you,' he says.

'I missed him too.'

'Did you make any new year's resolutions?'

'I don't know; I think I want to work out what to do with my life.'

He laughs. 'Well you can't exactly put it in a box and paint it purple, can you?'

'Maybe I'll read *Jude the Obscure*. Or pass my driving test.'

We sit together sipping our drinks and I want to tell him I feel like I'm spinning, that I'm struggling to be on my own, and sometimes the only time I feel anything at all is when I'm burning. Instead I ask how his fish and chips were, with Gabriella on Christmas Day.

'Tricky,' he says. 'I don't know that it ever gets easier. Just different, maybe. I'll be glad to have everyone back from the holidays. Did you get my present?'

I look away because I'd forgotten about his little pile of buttons.

'Ah,' he says. 'You didn't believe in me.'

'I'm sorry Frank; I just didn't know what to think about it –'

'Did you throw it away?' he asks.

'I threw it out of the window.'

I'm embarrassed and a bit ashamed, but Frank bursts out laughing.

'But that's perfect! Light and airy, I said. Out of the window is as light and airy as it gets.' He smiles at me. 'You shouldn't keep magic inside, anyway. Try your pocket.'

I put my hand into my pocket and find the buttons inside. I pull them out.

'Close your hands round them and shake,' he says.

I do, and when I open my hand again they've turned into pound coins. I laugh and shake my head at Frank.

'How did you do that?'

He pours me another cup of tea and it turns from blue to brown as he tips it into my mug. I realise I had stopped believing in him, and I'm glad to be back.

'So, what have you got planned for your January?' he asks.

'I'm starting up a choir, did I tell you?'

'No! Where's my invite?'

I laugh.

'It's at the school where one of my piano students goes. Her mum teaches there and asked me to do it. I'm thinking about getting them singing some Motown.'

'That's a great idea. I could come down and teach them some dance moves too.'

'Thanks, Frank. I'll bear that in mind.'

'Do! I'm almost as good at dancing as I am at drawing.'

He wiggles his feet from his chair in an attempt at a tap routine and I choke on my tea.

'I'm thinking about saving up to go away for a while too,' I say.

'That's not a bad idea. It does everyone a bit of good to see the world.'

'It feels like running away though. Do you think it is?'

'It might be. Or it could be running forwards. You don't even need to work it out; if you went and it was a mistake you could always come home again.'

'I guess.'

'There isn't really such a thing as a bad decision, Holly. If I'd thought there was I'd never have been able to get so good at dancing.'

I laugh at him.

'It's just that a lot of the time I really feel like I don't know anything. And I don't know why I'm doing any of the things I'm doing, and I have no idea what I want or how to achieve it. I feel panicked all the time.'

'Everyone feels like that,' he says. 'Have another biscuit.'

24

On Thursday that week – in between cleaning and a piano lesson – I go to the Jubilee Library. I ask the librarian where the atlases are and I sit with one on a purple bean bag, opening it on a map of the world. The library is too quiet though – there's no one else here – and I start to feel anxious. I phone Ellie but I guess she's working because she doesn't pick up, so I try a friend from London. She tells me I'm not supposed to talk in a library but there's no one here to mind so I ask her where she'd go if she wanted to escape. She says maybe Iceland.

'Holly, why don't you just come home? You don't need to run away again.'

'I didn't run away,' I say. 'I ran forwards. But I like the idea of Iceland, thanks. I'll speak to you soon, OK? Love you.'

I hang up and sit reading facts about the physical and economic geography of Iceland. Then it's time to head to my class, so I go and I teach it. I walk home afterwards, finding things I can count, like cars, or people wearing hats, and that way I don't have to be alone with nothing. It feels like there's an ant nest in my brain.

Later that evening I shave my legs and put red lipstick on. I go to the St James and sit at the bar drinking rum and eating prawn crackers. I talk to the guy who's working but it's his trial shift so he keeps getting distracted. Talking's not enough anyway; I need to touch someone. I finish my rum and cut down to the sea and walk along Madeira Drive and past the wheel and up to the entrance of the pier.

I look at it for a bit; the electric lights make me feel dizzy and I'd like to be upside down. I close my eyes and listen to the music and suck in the batter smell and the sugar and the noise of people being swung around. I want to move my own body though; I don't want to be flung through the air.

I light a cigarette and stand there looking at it. Then I walk down to the places that line the seafront. I wait in the queue for the Honey Club and slide in through the door, going straight to the bar. I stand for a while, watching the people around me. It's midnight already, and they sway, pushing their bodies together in time to the music: hands fumbling with new buttocks, groins hard against strange hips. I want to find something to hold.

I drink shots, quickly, neatly, and walk across the room looking for someone as lonely as me. Nobody is. A man with green eyes reaches out for my wrist and smiles like a Halloween lantern: eyes too bright. I smile back, let him take me to the bar and drink the vodka coke he gives me, open my mouth for his tongue. He's called Paul; he's funny and sexy and he can't dance. I dance for a bit anyway and he moves from foot to foot next to me. Then we drink some more vodka and kiss until I'm too hot in the club, and so we go and we lie on the stones on the beach. I don't care that it's cold. He gets on top of me and I can feel him getting hard. It's easier this time without a dragon watching so we get a cab back to his and I rub his crotch during the ride and he breathes in my ear. I don't feel anything but it doesn't hurt.

Later, after we've had sex on the sofa of the flat he shares with some other students, he cooks me an omelette because I say I'm hungry. He tells me his mum taught him to cook and that he still goes home most weekends. I eat the omelette and then we kiss some more and I go down on him, put him in my mouth and resist the urge to bite. I leave while he's sleeping and run home barefoot. I don't notice I've cut myself until the morning when I go to put my trainers on and find that my right foot is bruised and bloody.

25

Ellie and I go for a drink the next night. She asks me why I'm hobbling and I tell her I cut my foot swimming in the sea.

'Sweetheart, that's horrendous. You may have all kinds of fish shit in that wound; I hope you've cleaned it vigorously.'

I order food but she says she's already eaten. We sit there with our lies, and talk and drink and smoke a bit, and make each other feel better for a while.

26

The following Sunday afternoon Frank and I go to Gabriella's house. She makes a lamb curry while we bake, and they both test me sporadically on my copy of *The Highway Code*, which lies open on the kitchen surface by the oven.

The radio's on and Gabriella dances along. I want to sing but I feel too breathless, like I need to breathe in deeply just to keep on standing. It's my theory test next week and I'm worried because my brain seems to be jammed on fast forward. I can't focus on anything.

Frank and I are making clementine-and-ginger muffins and, combined with flat scents of lamb and erratic bursts of chilli and lime from the curry, the smells in the kitchen are thick and gorgeous.

I'm chopping the ginger and I ask Frank to pass a spoon to stir it into the mix.

'You're already holding one, you wally.'

I look down and the knife I had in my hand is a spoon. I don't know how Frank did it but when I look up he flicks some of the muffin dough at my face and I flick some back and we giggle. He looks so funny with raw cake on his face and I can't stop laughing. He hurls some at Gabriella too and I have to hold onto the side I'm laughing so much. Even after the others stop I don't; it makes my eyes run and I have to sit down and I'm still laughing and

Gabriella just puts her hand on the middle of my back and waits for me to finish.

I drive Frank home in his car and then walk the last bit back to mine: the boxes of muffins in my arms, ready for delivery to Jackie's cafe. Before I go Frank gives me a hug that lasts a long time, and when I get home I find a flower on my bed. I know it's his magic that put it there. He'd say it was mine, but I don't feel magic at all. I pull all the petals off. Then the flower's kind of sad and bald and I wish I'd just put it in a vase.

27

I need to know when things will feel safer, Sam. I need to know when I'll be able to find a space and just be able to be in it.

28

One of my piano students went to Barbados for Christmas and brought me back a little bracelet made of a leather cord with tiny cream shells. Even though they sell bracelets that are almost exactly the same in the shops along the front, it feels like a lucky charm next to the watch on my wrist.

I've brought my bike from home back to Brighton, strapped onto the back of the car. At the end of January Ellie, Danny, Duane, Mira, Sean and I cycle to the viaduct. We take picnics in our backpacks: flasks of hot coffee and sandwiches with thick slices of bread and the leftover Christmas ham my mum's filled my fridge with. As we cycle, the little bracelet jingles against my handlebars and I think about my fight with Frank, me needing to shout at someone under the arches, falling over in the mud. The jangly noise of the bracelet doesn't seem to be enough today either; I need to stretch my voice out too.

As the roads get quieter and calmer where it slowly becomes countryside, we speed up and Duane puts some music on, playing it out of speakers he's fixed into the side pockets of his backpack. Old 90s RnB tracks blare out into the trees which frame the road. We're embraced in the green cocoon of their stiff fingers. The branches bow slightly, their sharp needles held upright and alert to the beat. I'm glad the roads are empty; my mind can't focus on the grey space underneath me, the lines painted across it. I feel dangerous.

I like that you're dangerous, little kite.

We arrive tired and burning from the blood pumping close to our skin. We chain our bikes up and find a bench to sit and eat.

'That was a ridiculously hard cycle,' says Duane. 'I think I'm going to die.'

'Good,' says Mira. 'I'll eat your food.'

I laugh.

'Oh I see how it is, Holly; my adversity amuses you. I'll remember that next time you're in peril. I'll just laugh right in your face and see how you like it.'

'Peril?' says Ellie, 'We're not in a fucking Indiana Jones movie, Duane. You just need to stretch or something.'

'Yeah, I mean also I have the sandwiches,' I say. 'So you're probably going to want to be nice to me, or Mira will be getting your food.'

'Wow, what is this, let's all pick on Duane day? I brought the music guys; I'm the party.'

We unpack the food quickly and descend on it, swallowing big mouthfuls before we've done much chewing. Ellie takes out a wrapped-up sandwich and sits with it in front of her. She has a few bites and Sean holds her hand.

After we've eaten, we lie on thick picnic rugs, listening to the music and smoking. It's a freezing day but beautifully clear and the ground is dry and hard. Duane's brought a football and the boys have a kickabout while Mira and I pick at the leftover ham and Ellie lights up another cigarette. She's brought some research papers and sits with a biro and a highlighter decoding them. Mira and I flick through the Saturday papers, arguing with the articles and agreeing with each other. I can't tell you what we say, just that we keep talking; there's noise, the cold, the ground beneath me. At one point Mira asks me if I'm OK and I say, 'I feel like there's a bit of me that's somewhere else; does that make sense to you?'

Ellie looks at me.

'Darling, you've never made sense. It's your air of mystery that makes you so very alluring.'

Then she laughs and throws some ham at my face.

'Obviously I'm joking, babe. Have another bit of pig. Life's just fucking hard, isn't it? Sometimes we're manic. Sometimes we may as well be dead. You need to do some yoga or something; this picnic rug's got no feng shui.'

Mira shrugs at me and shakes her head.

'Ellie's always so useful and sensitive, isn't she?'

It isn't really warm enough to be sitting, so after a while we get up and join the game. We play three-a-side – Duane, Mira and me versus Sean, Ellie and Danny – with jumpers and backpacks for goalposts. It's pretty haphazard and the ball smacks into our feet and bounces off with sporadic aim and little skill but it feels good to be running around. All I have to be aware of is my body moving, and the grass, and the ball. Sometimes when I kick it I think about conkers exploding, but then I run around a bit and remember we're people not pigeons, and someone passes me the ball and I'm back in my body again.

The score is 5-all and Danny suggests the next goal be the winner. We immediately ramp up the pace, shooting more often and diving down in front of the goal to ward off opposing balls. Eventually Duane catches the ball on the side of his head and aims it down to Mira who crosses it to me in front of the goal. I don't have that much skill on the ground and Danny's coming towards me so I have to shoot right away or we'll lose possession. I push it forward hard, just slipping it in past the left post, and Duane and Mira jump on top of me, celebrating our sudden victory.

As we scooch back over to start packing up for the cycle home I clench my jaw. I turn away for a minute to hold my face in my hands and close my eyes.

I wonder whether every time I feel good there'll be a part of my tongue or my thighs or the dead ends where my hair frays slightly at the bottom that's somewhere else with you.

29

I wish I'd made more of an effort to speak French to you. I liked it in the mornings when you'd roll over and tell me about your dreams in French, even though I didn't really understand you. It always sounded a little bit dirty. I feel stupid I never asked you to teach me more. I think about trying to learn Yemba too. English sounds dry in the mouths around me, like dead wood.

Sometimes when I sit in my room and miss you I try speaking French; I feel like the extra effort I'm making might mean my words somehow reach you. I think that if I go somewhere everyone speaks French the chances of you hearing me would be magnified. I could sit under *le ciel* and whisper, *Tu me manques. Je t'aime.*

And I want to shout at you too, in English. Tell you how you've turned me into something empty: an eggshell broken in the trash, the sound of electricity cutting out. In my mouth you are a word I want to throw up but you cling to my gums like blood.

30

We cycle back to Brighton together and then split off to go our separate ways home. Duane says he's left something at Mira's so they go back together and Ellie and Sean are going the same way anyway so Danny says he'll walk me back to mine. I laugh at him for thinking I need walking anywhere, but I'm grateful for the company. We get off our bikes and push them.

'I'm glad you came back after Christmas, Holly,' he says. 'We didn't know if you would.'

'Ellie said that too.'

'Well we are. You're part of the group now.'

He reaches over and squeezes my shoulder and looks like he's trying to decide whether to keep talking or not.

'I've never met anyone like you, Holly. You kind of just open yourself up to things and let them hurt if they need to.'

I sit at home that night reading a book my parents have given me about grief. I look out of the window at my sliver of the sea and feel scared. Things sometimes feel like they're starting to get solid around me but at the edge of every day is a shadowy bit I know I might fall into, where I won't wash my hair for weeks, or where I'll scratch my skin until it bleeds, or run until I'm sick, or lie flat on the floor of my room until the tears make my skin sore. Sometimes I think I've fallen into it already, or that I'm always falling and always trying to climb back out.

This is what you've left me with, Sam, and I'm angry with you. My book says this is normal. I'd like to write to the author and ask if it's normal for me to want to claw at your skin, but I think she'd just refer me to chapter two where it says that grief is unpredictable and I should allow myself to express my emotions in any healthy way I can.

I can't think about any of this tonight. I feel hot and jittery. I want to be blank and numb.

I don't know how I get down to the beach. When I'm there I take off my clothes and I go for a swim. I climb up out of the water when I'm crying so much I can't breathe. I can't feel the place the sobs are coming from. I'm frozen.

31

The air is thick and white. If it were London, I'd say it was going to snow. Here it just rains, soggy and ripe and cold. The starlings have gone. The seagulls blend into the air; it's all feathers and blank eyes and sludge in between. Round beyond the marina, on the walk towards Saltdean, the waves slap harder and faster up against the wall and onto the path. On the tourist beach, the other side of the pier, it's just empty space. The weekends are quiet: no one eating candy floss or feeding chips to the birds. The stones on the beach are wet. I am battered by winter. I look at the sea and imagine it tearing me apart.

32

On Wednesday I deliver cakes to Jackie's cafe then sit in the corner with my morning coffee, jumbling up plans for my piano lesson later with the meanings of road signs and markings. I didn't sleep well again the night before and I can feel a stiffness in my skin. I can tell it won't go until the caffeine's kicked in and I'm several rooms into cleaning Mrs Almeidy's house. My phone buzzes.

Really sorry guys, I can't make the quiz tonight. See you soon. Danny

I'm sure there's a good reason for it but he really helps us out in the sports round and we'll definitely struggle without him so it isn't ideal, and it's probably too late for us to find someone else. Plus he's always the person we take the piss out of when we get stuff wrong. I say goodbye to Jackie and head out, reasoning in my mind that it's the book club next week. I'll see him then. It's raining again.

We win the quiz that night by three points. Ellie and Duane smash the sports round – they've been reading up – and we play our joker on current affairs and get full marks. I feel particularly smug as I answer a question about Iceland I learnt from the atlas.

Mira and Duane go to get drinks for us all afterwards and I

ask Ellie if she knows why Danny couldn't come. She says she isn't sure and I say maybe he'd had a fight with Mira. She looks at me questioningly.

'Aren't they sort of together?' I ask.

Sean glances over and at us. 'Mira and Danny? What planet are you living on? She and Duane have been seeing each other since last time we won. Had you honestly not noticed?'

I look at Ellie who smiles and shrugs. I try to find my lip balm in my bag. Ellie leans in and says, 'Danny's definitely single.'

I'm pretty drunk by the time we leave; I'm glad I don't have far to get home. In my room I take off my clothes and chuck them on the floor by my desk. I still haven't got a chair – the room is exactly as I found it: a bed and a desk and a chest of drawers. Ellie's told me it needs things on the walls but I like it bare. It's too small to feel empty.

I don't feel sleepy at all. The alcohol's made me feel kind of turned on. I haven't been able to come since you died and I don't know if I can be bothered to try tonight. I always end up crying. There's a chapter on sex and grief in my book, and it tells me to use a mirror when I masturbate. There's a mirror on my desk; I use it to do my make-up, so I take off my pants and lie on the floor. There's no lampshade on my light and the bulb hangs above me shining dimly. It's trying so hard to make the room bright that I feel kind of sorry for it. I hold the mirror with one hand and watch the other one between my legs. I move it around a bit and slow down my breathing. But I'm cold without a duvet wrapped around me; I just feel lonely.

I get up and put my pants back on. I walk to the window and sit on the windowsill. I press my face against the glass. It's wet and cold against my skin and I roll my head slowly, squashing my nose and lips along its surface. I open my mouth so my teeth are touching the glass too and push against it a bit. I notice that I'm shivering. They rattle against the window. I sink back, looking at the smudge of oil and make-up. They smear across my view of the streetlights and the night.

I think about how hard I'd have to push for my teeth to fall out. I think about you: the smooth curves of your face, your high forehead and your mouth, open and laughing, showing your one twisted tooth in the bottom row. The tiny scar above your left eyebrow. Your mouth. It hurts. I push my forehead into the window again and put my phone against my lips like it's your tongue. I open my mouth and wedge the phone inside. I can feel its plastic edge jutting into my teeth and wonder what would happen if I bit on it. I don't know if it would break or if I would.

33

It's Jackie's turn to host the book club. We meet in her flat above the cafe and talk about *Chocolat*. She makes roast chicken and apple crumble. Frank sends a message to say he has a migraine and can't come. It feels flat without him and I worry about him, ill and on his own.

Afterwards, Ellie and I go back to Danny's to drink whisky. His flat's in Hove, up on the seventh floor of a block on the seafront. We go out onto the balcony and watch the darkness moving where the sea is, listen to it purr.

The whisky tastes of petrol to me, so Danny gives me wine instead. Sean comes to meet us and we sit outside with music playing through the window and blankets to keep us warm. Danny has a guitar and I ask if I can play it. It feels warm and familiar. We sit there and I sing and every now and then a seagull flies past or we smell a gush of salt on the wind. I play covers and take requests and everyone sings along. Ellie asks me to play something of my own.

'I don't know if I'll remember anything,' I say. 'It's been a while.'

I do remember, and when it makes my eyes well up Danny puts his arm around me and I lean against his chest playing the love song I wrote for you. It should be confusing but it isn't, until I put my coat on and go to say goodbye and feel like I want to kiss him. I don't know if the others notice but Danny looks at me for a bit too long, and I have to look away and go home very quickly.

34

You are a worn out house I walk around in. I try to imagine another kind of home.

35

February 12th is Shrove Tuesday. I go round to Frank's for breakfast and he makes a giant jug of batter. We fill pancake after pancake with lemon and sugar and golden syrup and fruit and ice cream. We make them wide and flat in his frying pan and hurl them into the air to turn them.

When a pancake is flipped there's an exact moment when it's

suspended between one way down and the other way up. Frank chucks one into the air and it seems to stop and hang there. Then he jiggles the pan and it falls back out of the sky the other way round.

'That moment there,' he says, 'that in between; it's OK just to be still in that sometimes.'

36

Do pancakes feel like astronauts do in zero gravity? Do you know that you don't exist anymore? Do you miss me too, Sam?

37

At the house I clean on Tuesdays no one is ever in. I have my own key and there's always a mug and a tea bag out for me on the side with a cheque. I've only met the lady who owns it once when she interviewed me. Beyond that I only know what I've pieced together from the house. It's completely spotless with no clutter or clues to help me. All the drawers and wardrobes are kept locked shut and the rooms have mirrors where I'd expect pictures to be.

I've got used to it, but at first it made me feel uncomfortable. Walking on the cream carpet in my socks I felt like I was the first person making prints in the sand after the tide's gone out. I wear plain clothes to work there and put my phone on silent because if I don't it makes me jump when it rings. The ceiling in the hall is high, and there is a round clock on the wall that looks like it should tick but it doesn't.

It's a blue-sky day: cold but sunny, like the winter is slowly letting go. Outside, shop fronts belt out music, and the people milling around clutch cups of tea that seep heat into their hands and make them feel hopeful.

Inside, the house makes me furious. I switch the lights on in every room and hoover the floor as though I want to bruise it, sucking the carpet hard with the nozzle and slapping it down again. I push it into the skirting boards, making it thump. The house pushes back. We're hurting each other.

I go upstairs and sit on the bathroom floor. The tall window opposite the bath lets the sky in. From inside, the blueness looks blank and heavy. I take off my socks and put my feet down on the bathroom tiles. They're cold. I look around at the barren room: the bath sat empty like a huge stomach; the curtains light, like they should twitch and jerk in the slightest breeze. The house is always comatose though; they hang limp.

A fly groans somewhere near the back corner of the room and I feel like the air is dry enough to crack. I can smell the cleaning products I've poured into the sink and the toilet, that I've used to scrub the bath. I stand up and put my feet into the tub, switching on the tap and letting water wash over them, climbing up the ankles of my jeans. I sit down on the edge of the bath, take off my clothes and slip in. I lie there on my back with my knees up like I'm giving birth. I haven't put the plug in and the water mostly drains away but small puddles linger, and nestle in my pubic hair.

I lie there – angry – and for a good few minutes I think about touching myself. I want to come in that cream house where I don't feel like a person, and I move my hand down my stomach and between my legs. I start to move my fingers slowly but I'm tired and I have to put the hoover away. I sit up and turn the tap off. The water drains away but I stay sat there. I'm damp now, and it's cold. Then I get out slowly and pat myself dry with the hand towel. It's thick and luxurious; it makes me feel worn away.

In the bathroom mirror, I'm surprised I still look the same. I thought maybe I'd be smaller, or more see-through. I don't look different, Sam, but my skin doesn't feel anything except the cold anymore, and I think I'm disappearing. I'm scared, and something in me wants to push against it, to move faster than is safe. I want to find places outside my body where I can sit and be nothing except the wind and the grip of someone else's hands. I'll find them in a bar; I'll know them because they'll be lonely like mine are: looking for a body to remember how to feel with, touching everything a bit too hard.

I'll pinch my skin between fingers until it's blue like water is, when it lies flat beneath the sky. I'll lie flat beneath a stranger and be nothing but limbs.

I need to finish up so I clean the bathroom again. Then I switch off all the lights and start to walk home. I choose a road that I don't know and then take every first left turn until I'm lost. Sometimes there isn't a left turn for a while, and I start to jog, like I need to find one soon. I don't know where I'm going. I think I want to turn back; I'm tired, and this game seems to have gone on for too long. I want to be still in the air like Frank's pancake. At some point I find a pub and I go in, and I order a bottle of wine that I drink on my own. I order a whisky coke and then another and then I'm in a taxi I think someone else must have phoned for me, and the driver asks me where I want to go. She's a woman, and I find that surprising. I ask her to take me down to the sea. She asks which bit, and I say wherever's nearest. When she drops me off she won't let me pay, and she gets out of the cab and asks if I'm OK. I look at her. I want to ask her for a hug.

'Is there anyone I can phone for you?' she asks.

So I give her your number and she rings it.

'It's just cutting out,' she says. 'Are you sure you got it right?'

I run away from her then, as fast as I can, down to the sea and along the front. I climb over the groynes and keep running until I know where I am. Then I sit and stare at the water.

In the morning I'm hungover and covered in scratches. I go to the bathroom, and kneel in front of the toilet. When I'm sick, I wonder if letting go always has to hurt this much. I don't want to let go of you though, Sam. I don't want to let you go.

38

I always forget that winter seeps into the days you expect to be spring; that the beginning of March is an extension of February's white gazpacho skies: chilled and bitter. Even the sea is quiet. Everyone's tired.

I pass my driving test on 2nd March, in a week that fitfully spurts warmth, as though the weather is fighting its own monotony. Frank takes me for a celebratory drive on the Saturday, and we go back to his house for hot chocolate with Ellie and Sean. It's a cold day and Frank lends me the cream-and-brown jumper he's always wearing. He tells me he's just finished knitting a new one so I should keep it, that young people never wear enough clothes anymore anyway.

'I feel like I'll turn into you if I wear this though, Frank,' I say. 'Suddenly a pack of biscuits will burst out from one of the sleeves.'

The four of us sit around chatting, and Frank tells us a story about a magic show in Berlin where his hat had accidentally caught fire. Everyone'd thought it was part of the act and they'd all gone wild for it, so he'd decided to keep it in.

'Ian was furious the first time it happened though; he thought I'd added a fire trick to the show without telling him. Then we started to try and catch each other out every time, adding sneaky bits into the routine.'

'So what you're telling me is it's not biscuits I should worry about in this jumper but catching on fire. Thanks, Frank; I'm not sure I want it anymore.'

'Have you ever played any good pranks, Holly?' Sean asks me.

'I don't know.' I think about it. 'Sam came home really, really drunk once, so when I woke up in the morning I turned everything upside down in our room to try and freak him out. But he was kind of too hungover to notice so it didn't really work until the evening when he went to get something out of a drawer and it was the wrong way up. He was so confused though, it was just kind of feeble and I felt sorry for him.'

We laugh. I'm surprised by the story, even as I tell it. I guess I don't talk about you that much. There's no one here who'd know how funny you were when you were hungover: kind of squishy and perplexed, when normally you were so self-assured. I think about our friends, who would've got it. They've mostly stopped calling since I didn't see any of them at Christmas. I feel so far from home, and it's how I wanted it, but I'm suddenly sad.

I go to help Frank wash up the mugs in the kitchen. I pass him one to put away, but when I turn around he's leaning on the kitchen counter with his eyes closed.

'Are you OK, Frank?'

He looks up and out the window, where a sparrow takes off from a tree outside. He smiles and whistles to it. He looks at me looking at him and says, 'Well it's rude not to say hello, don't you think?'

He takes the mug from me and I decide not to push it, but before we go I ask him if he's had any more migraines.

'Only when I eat too much cheese,' he says. He wafts us out of the door. 'Look after my jumper, Holly. Stay warm.'

39

This morning the sea was completely flat with thin stripes running across it like pyjamas. The sky was white with a bit of grey underneath it, and the day felt like it was aching. I wondered if the seagulls were bored with being the same colour as the sky.

Now it's evening and the sun is out on my right-hand side and the sea in front of me is glowing. It's patchy: blue in parts, silver in others, and it looks like the light's underneath it, pushing up through the water like it's determined to be seen. I sit on the beach with an ice cream.

To my left the white cliffs glow like teeth. The sea curls; there's still no foam to the waves but they're rising up and rolling into themselves like they're lungs, keeping the world alive.

40

It's Sunday. Gabriella and I are cooking. We're watching *Hunger*, and the rain is whipping up a playground for slugs outside the window. Not long after the film starts Gabriella stops what she's doing. We sit still and watch it through to the end.

When it's finished we both turn back to the hob and when the meal's ready we sit down to eat together. It feels like there's something in the air we're both still trying to unpick, like a knot in one of Frank's balls of wool.

'What did you think of it?' I ask.

'It was beautiful,' she says. 'But quite brutal too.'

She gets two mugs out of the cupboard and starts to make tea.

'I don't know. It sort of hit a bit of a nerve. I can relate to some of the stuff in it, you know. That sense of having to fight from a place of being seen in a certain way, of being perceived as inherently bad or wrong and everything being stacked up against you. It was painful in that way.'

I take the tea as she passes it over.

'Thanks.' I add some milk and get up to find a teaspoon from the drawer.

'I don't know,' she continues. 'I think it was also partly about the way history shifts our perspectives.'

'What do you mean?'

'Well, I guess in terms of how our identities position us in relation to others, and how that changes over time, maybe? Like, there are so many people I love who are white but who are part of this history that makes me angry. About where I'm from, what my ancestors went through. That's difficult sometimes, and it's complicated.'

'The bit that confused me was the part when the priest was talking about negotiation, about it being preferable to suicide or fighting. I didn't know whose side we were meant to be on.'

'I don't think we were meant to be on a side,' she says. 'It's what Sands says; life and our experiences have focused our beliefs differently. I know that life can change drastically for the better with a push from the right person at the right time, but if not, in a situation like that, maybe all there is is dying.'

'You sound like Danny.'

She laughs. 'We think the same way sometimes. It was interesting – that conversation between Sands and the priest – what they said about terrorists –'

'I don't know if I believe there's such a thing as a terrorist anymore, Gabby. I think maybe there are just different types of hate, or power, or whatever it is –'

'Right. But as long as people are taught to be scared of other people there'll be terrorists; that's what terror creates.' She reaches for another spoonful of sugar. 'You just have to question who's creating that fear. Whether it's coming from what's supposed to be our side or what's supposed to be theirs. And, like I say, I don't really know who "our side" is. History hasn't always put me on the same team as it would like to now.'

'Can we be on the same team?' I ask.

She laughs. 'Yeah, we can be on the same team.'

We clear up slowly and I hug her goodbye. As I walk down the road my mind's on Ellie. I don't know what it feels like for your body to starve. I can imagine the pain but I feel like there must be some will to keep living, despite the high from controlling your body so tightly and riding the hunger out. I can see Ellie's illness hurting her, but I can understand wanting to turn your body against itself, making it go numb.

41

You used to laugh when I got upset about films or books or stuff I'd read in the news. Sometimes you'd kiss me. Other days, you'd tease me; you'd tell me I used it for catharsis, that I'd sit and get upset over other people's bad stuff in order to let my own sadness out.

You'd said that that was what I was doing the day the boy on the bus called you the N-word. You told me I was being selfish, that crying wouldn't solve anything and my empathy was self-gratifying. You were upset. You said I should be angry or pragmatic but not sad. We had got off the bus and were about ten minutes from home.

You said, 'Don't cry about things you can walk away from. There are people who can't switch off their shit when you decide you're fed up with feeling it.'

I knew it was about the boy on the bus and not about me. I could tell you didn't want to talk so we just walked. When we got to the front door, you'd taken my hand and we kept on walking. We went down onto the Thames Path behind the flat and walked until we found a bench. I didn't know what to say, so I told you that. I asked how you were feeling.

'Tired,' you said.

After a bit, we talked about other stuff: the film we'd just seen, what we were going to eat that night, and you tucked me in under your arm and held me there. We didn't speak about it again until the next morning. I'd brought us coffee to have in bed, and you sipped yours and kissed me.

'I didn't really sleep. I kept thinking about that boy yesterday. No one has said that to me in a long time.'

'Do you want to talk about it?'

'Not exactly. It just upset me. And it upset you too but, you know, we're upset in different ways, from different places, and that's all I was trying to say to you yesterday.'

'Yeah. I was upset because I love you but someone was attacking you; of course it's different.'

'Right, and for something that's always there, that I'm always thinking about. That's why I get angry.'

'I know. I just don't know how to help you in those moments.'

'Yeah. I guess we just have to keep talking about it. You're white, Holly, and I'm black, and that's not going anywhere. I love you and this stuff is always going to be a thing.'

'We just have to keep talking about it.'

'Yes.'

Walking home from Gabriella's, I think about that conversation, and the ones that came after. Over the next few weeks, we started talking more about racism, about how it was for you to live in a racist world. We talked about our kids, the way people would see them, the things they might experience that I didn't understand. We talked about what being white felt like for me, about how I'd never really had to think about that.

You always made me laugh so much, Sam, even when we

talked about things that feel hard. We'd start talking about what we wanted the world to look like for our kids and suddenly we'd be laughing about something ridiculous, like you wanting to call one of them Horatio. And we'd still be talking about the hard stuff, but I'd be smiling at you, and you'd have your arms round me, and we'd be excited about the future, even though things aren't always easy.

It hurts so much we never got to make those plans happen, Sam. I know that – whatever Gabriella and I said – when it comes to the ways we're racialised, the teams we're on can never be straightforward. But I miss you, Sam; I miss being your team-mate so much.

42

It's Friday evening and I feel reckless. I want to run or dance or do something with my body, but I don't know how to use it right. I try sitting on my bed and reading, but my mind isn't playing with my muscles and I need to be on my feet.

You understood this feeling. You'd say, 'Let's get a train some-where, find a new city to love.' We'd have packed pants and a toothbrush. I'd have made a picnic of cheese and beers and chicken wings and we'd have sat on a train and played cards and gone on an adventure.

Tonight, I think about shaving my hair off or making myself sick.

I get a text from Danny, asking if I want to go for a drink. I say yes and meet him at the St James. I put on a bra under my top, and some lipstick, and go out without a coat. I walk across the road and down the hill and Danny's sitting in the pub. I feel relieved to see him. His smile sits calm in his eyes and he's reassuringly broad.

We order hot rum and he asks if I know how to play chess. I do, so he gets the chessboard down from the games shelf. He's not very good; he calls his knights horses and keeps forgetting that pawns take diagonally.

'How can you be this bad? It was your idea to play. You're worse at chess than you are at pub quizzes.'

'Oh, and you're so great, are you?'

I take his queen and put him in check.

'I knew you were going to do that; it's part of my long-term plan.'

'Right, sure.'

'No seriously, I'm lulling you into a false sense of security.'

'Nah, mate. The long-term plan is you're going down.'

I move my castle in line with his king.

'Checkmate.'

'What? How did you do that?'

'I'm pretty stealthy.'

He laughs.

'You're the least stealthy person I know. You couldn't tell a lie even if there was a pork pie at stake.'

I laugh at him. We talk about work and music, and drink some more. I have that wild feeling again, like I need to find someone to spend the night with, touching too hard and not feeling anything. But Danny wouldn't be able to kiss me like I wasn't there. I don't know if he can tell that I'm thinking about kissing him and I'm worried it's gone too far already, so I say I have to leave. He catches my hand as I stand up.

'Holly, are you OK?'

I nod, 'I'm just tired.'

The rain is really heavy and it's only a couple of minutes up the road but by the time I get home I'm soaking. I can barely turn the key in the door my fingers are so slippery, and I'm drunk.

The red numbers on the clock by my bed say 12.42 and I sit down and imagine what would have happened if I'd brought Danny back. I wring my trousers out in the sink to dry them. Then I lie in bed and think about kissing him, his scratchy chin making my skin red in the morning. I think about how good it might have been to fall asleep in the hair that pokes out the top of his T-shirt, cramped into my single bed and curled round him. My head is itchy where my hair is wet between the pillow and my scalp, and I think about your hands on my body and the way we moved into each other. I put my back against the wall but it's cold. It doesn't feel at all like you did.

43

Ellie phones me one morning. Her viva is done; she's finished her PhD. I call in sick to my cleaning jobs and take her out for a late breakfast. We go to the Mercure hotel and drink champagne that we can't afford but neither of us cares. We spend the day mooching round North Laine and eat fish and chips on the pier for lunch. In the sea there are four people swimming together; they're doing front crawl, arms turning in the water like blades at a wind farm.

We eat with our fingers and when Ellie can't finish hers I eat it for her. The batter around the edge of the fish is a perfect amber and only oozes oil after its crisp is split by teeth. We smother our chips in ketchup and my fingers smell sweet all afternoon. We talk about her work and I don't understand much of it but I'm proud of her. She's been offered a position in the department and she's going to stay on.

'Have I got to call you Dr Ellie now?' I ask.

'Absolutely; it's the only thing I'll answer to.'

We walk back into town and when he finishes work, Sean comes and meets us at The Hop Poles for a few beers. I half expect Danny to come too but he doesn't. Sean looks at me and says, 'Look, Holly, I want to say something that may seem a bit weird.'

'You are a bit weird.'

'Well, your face is a bit weird.'

We laugh. Ellie rolls her eyes and kicks Sean.

'What did you want to say?' she asks. 'Spit it out, boy.'

He looks at her and then at me. 'I think you may know this already, Holly, but Danny really likes you.'

I don't say anything. Ellie frowns at Sean, like she doesn't think he should have said it. She turns to me apologetically.

'Look, Sam died nine months ago and I know you think you're a mess. For what it's worth you seem like a normal level of mess to me but I know it's confusing so please just be careful. Mr DeVito is a nice boy and we all love you both a lot.'

I look at her. 'We don't have to talk about it,' she continues. 'Sean shouldn't have brought it up. But if you want to . . .'

I nod and we get another drink, and afterwards I walk home, trying to work out how all of the things I'm feeling sit together.

It's hard, so I start to run, and when I get home I'm tired enough and drunk enough to sleep.

44

I've written a new song about you. It's about the holiday we had in Rome: the night we sat up together in a little bar drinking coffee and smoking. We walked to the Spanish Steps, which is what people who are in love are supposed to do. I bought a rose from a street seller and gave it to you and you laughed at me and said they were meant to be for the women. I tucked it behind your ear and kissed your neck and your ear lobe and your ear. You just held me and breathed deeply and then we found the cafe round the corner where we sat and watched the sun come up and looked at each other and felt like we could stay there forever. You wrote me dirty messages on a napkin and I stroked your thigh under the table.

I don't know how to put the song to music; I haven't been able to find a melody that's beautiful and sad enough yet.

45

I'm hosting the March book club and because I only rent a small room, I borrow Frank's kitchen and hold it there. I make home-made lamb burgers with mint and coriander, a spicy yellow-tomato relish and a crumbling raspberry-and-white-chocolate pavlova. I've chosen *Vile Bodies* by Evelyn Waugh and am nervous about whether the others will like it. I spend ages deciding what to wear and stand under the shower worrying while the food cooks.

After my shower I sit on the toilet, wrapped in my towel and dripping on the burnt-red tiles of Frank's bathroom, flicking through a book of poetry from the shelf above the loo. Frank has a record on downstairs. It's Vladimir Ashkenazy playing Chopin's Nocturne in C-sharp Minor and my fingers move slightly as they feel the key patterns flex through the air.

Noel arrives just as I come downstairs, and we stand in the kitchen waiting for the kettle to boil as the others duck out of the rain and through the front door. Jackie's glasses steam up and everyone piles their wet coats over the radiator in the hall. The rain is falling in sheets like cling film and they're all drenched. Cups of tea are poured and plates of food dished out, and we all squeeze in around the table in Frank's kitchen. Gabriella smiles at me as I hand her a burger. I watch as she tries it and she nods her approval as she dips a forkful into the relish.

We argue over the book. Ellie says that it's over-written, that she didn't care about any of the characters and that it's cynical but without anywhere to aim its cynicism. Danny says it's empty on purpose and that's the point; you're meant to laugh at it, and Gabriella joins in on his side as I get up to put the kettle on. Danny is sat diagonally opposite me at the table and I feel more aware of my face than normal but otherwise nothing seems different. When he speaks I avoid eye contact and occasionally I look at the ceiling, which is painted white and has little cracks in the corners. I wait for the kettle to boil. Noel says he doesn't think it's empty and that the holes in the characters are the most important bits. He says he thinks it trivialises despair, which is problematic, and I bring the tea back to the table and Ellie says she found it unpleasantly artificial and if that was deliberate then it worked but she wasn't sure she'd liked it. I say I think the book is funny. Gabriella agrees and says she thinks that's the point Danny's making. I put the back of my fingers to my cheeks to cool down my face, and try to relax my shoulders by puffing a little bit of air out and eating a mouthful of pavlova to give my mouth something to do.

I go up to the roof to smoke with Ellie after everyone has finished eating. It's a clear night with a bit of a wind and from within the hood of my coat I'm getting wafts of Frank's shampoo in my hair. It smells of pears and makes me feel clean. I draw on my cigarette and listen to a seagull in the distance.

'That piano music Frank was playing when we got here; what was it, poppet?' Ellie asks.

'Chopin.'

'I thought it might be. Noel told me once that Frank plays Chopin when he's stuck on something. I didn't know what he meant so I asked Frank about it and he told me he always listens to it if he's working on a very tricky knitting pattern. I don't know; it's not like Frank to be facetious so maybe he meant it but I always felt like there was more to it. He seems alright to me though?'

'Yeah, I think so. He loves these nights.'

I yawn and she pokes her finger into the hole it makes in my mouth, jerking it back before I close it again. I laugh.

'You weirdo.'

'I remember when I first met Frank,' she says. 'I sat down opposite him in Jackie's cafe and he looked up, stared at me and said, 'You look ill. Is someone looking after you?' I was really thrown by it; this old man I didn't know just going there.'

'He's got a way about him, hasn't he?'

'I didn't know what the fuck to say but then he showed me this article he was reading in *National Geographic* about manatees –'

'Manatees?'

'Yeah; they're sea cows: massive mammals that live in rivers. We must have talked for an hour or so, bits about manatees and bits about me or him, and then he lent me a book – I can't even remember what it was – and he told me about this book club, told me to come. I wasn't sure about it, but I went – obviously – and, I don't know, it's really helped.'

'Frank seems to have a knack of finding people who need him, doesn't he?'

She stubs out her cigarette butt in the ashtray Frank keeps on the roof and steps away from me, spinning around with her arms held up like a ballet dancer.

'We all need each other, darling,' she says. 'It's a crazy vicious world and each other's all we've got. You done?'

I squash the end of my cigarette and nod.

'I want to go dancing. What do you reckon, after this?'

She wiggles her eyebrows at me.

'Let's do it! We haven't been out in ages. I'll call the others and get them to meet us down the front.'

I could have gone by myself, danced until someone caught me, been alone with someone else for a while. I don't want to do that tonight.

46

Sometimes you clog my daytimes. Sometimes you are the only way I can breathe. Sometimes I think it might be getting better, but night always rolls round again, or daytime, or night again.

47

We dance until the club closes and it's just us and a bunch of students. We're crazy to be doing this on a Wednesday night but by the time we leave we're drunk enough we can't feel the cold.

The wetness of the sky is like a flannel. It's raining in that way that makes the air damp as you walk through it. It falls in sheets – thin and constant – mixing into the sea without a splash. It's always fucking raining here, Sam; you'd go mad from it.

By the shore, Ellie and Sean flag down a taxi and split from us, heading home. The rest of us are still buzzing from the alcohol and the dancing. We're hungry, so we decide to get toasties from the little kiosk on the prom. Duane's is ham and tomato. I warn him toasted tomato gets really hot and he says the ham will cool it down. I find that convincing and order the same, but it doesn't work and I burn my mouth. He laughs at me as I poke my tongue out and try to cool it down with the rain.

We duck down onto the beach. It's slippery. We sit on the stones, coats underneath our bums to stop our trousers from getting wet. We sit looking at the moon. The sandwiches are thick and sweaty. Where the bread has been toasted the crusts crunch together. It leaves my fingers smelling of oil. Someone says something about work in the morning.

'We're too old for this.'

Duane leans over and bites off a chunk of Mira's sandwich, jumps up and pulls her to her feet. 'You're right. Come on; let's get going. I feel like we won't be thanking you and Ellie for this in the morning.'

I laugh.

'See you.'

They leave. I look at Danny and realise how cold I'm getting. We stand up. The sea doesn't look wet in the darkness and I want to touch it. Sometimes it feels like we've been flipped around: me and the water and the sky. The sea could be space and the sky could be the silky cover of a planet I'd like to be on. I'd stroke its navy-blue breathing. I could put a star in my mouth and set myself on fire from the inside. *Je voudrais te regarder respirer pendant que tu dors, te voir inspirer le ciel.*

All I can see is the sea, close up, full of the dark. I turn and face Danny.

'Do you want me to walk you home?' he asks.

'I think I can probably manage on my own,' I say, and I laugh again.

'That's not exactly what I meant though.'

I look at him in the rain. He's wearing a dark-green anorak and his hair is stuck to his forehead, water dripping down his nose. I take a step forward and put my hands on his hips. He puts one of his hands on my waist and the other one under my chin and I'm very aware of my breathing. He kisses me. It's so tentative it makes me want to cry. It's like he doesn't want to hurt me and that's what makes it hurt. I'm real to him and he's funny and kind and I put my arms right round him and let him wrap me up. I don't think he knows he's holding me together, that if he let go I'd fall apart.

We stop kissing and then we look at each other for a bit and I don't know what to do so I say, 'Goodnight, Danny.'

I untangle myself from him and turn to go home. I don't look back at him but I want to. I'm so sorry, Sam. I start to run, and as I reach the path I nearly slip.

Spring

I'm a bag of bones
wrapped up in skin. Hold me; let
me be like water.

1

Brighton is tired and damp, like it's been left screwed up in a washing machine, unable to dry because of the chill.

I still sleep in your jumper most nights but sometimes – if I'm very tired – I forget to put it on. This makes me feel guilty.

2

It's Sunday so I've gone to Gabriella's. She opens the door, looks at me and says, 'I'm going to run you a bath, Holly. Then we're going to cook.'

I guess I look as tired as I feel. I don't argue with her. I sit in the hot water and curl into myself. Afterwards I put the warm socks she's given me over my tights and go downstairs.

'So, what are we making today?'

'I thought we might get you cooking pastry. What do you reckon?'

'Sure, sounds good.'

Words are an effort but I say some things anyway to make

me seem normal. Gabriella knows this so she puts on the radio and dances.

'You're looking quite glam, Gabby.'

She's had her hair done in a pile of braids stacked on top of her head in a thick knot. She spins around underneath them, gets ingredients out from the cupboards with strong hands. She dances like she's liquid.

'Thanks. I'm going on a date tonight. Don't look so surprised. You're not the only one with a social life, young lady. He's a doctor I met in London over New Year. We're going wine tasting.'

'What am I doing here?' I say. 'Don't you want to be getting ready?'

'Doing what? I'm not going to sit around painting my toenails.'

I smile. Gabriella turns the radio up and 'Atomic' by Blondie blares out. She says, 'It's funny; I had my first kiss with Joseph's father to this song in 1995. We were at a roller disco and he was standing on the middle of the dance floor without any skates on. I remember thinking he must've been a bit of an idiot, but then when I skated past him he grabbed my arm. I was wearing these ankle socks with tiny penguins on and he told me he liked them. We got chatting and I asked him why he wasn't skating. He said he liked to stand still; he *was* a bit of an idiot to be honest, but he was very handsome and when this song came on he kissed me.'

'Where is he now?' I ask.

'I don't know,' she replies. 'We're not in touch.'

We make a lattice pie with chicken and peas inside and a slightly soggy bottom. Gabriella tells me it isn't bad for my first attempt. We sit and eat it with broccoli for a late lunch and she doesn't ask me any questions. She just tells me to come over any time I want. She says the weather's been rubbish and everyone's a bit down. It'll get better now it's spring.

I don't tell her I kissed Danny. I don't tell her I want to wake up and see another person's face on my pillow. I don't tell her I'm so lonely I feel bent over with it; it rattles in my breath.

After we've eaten she says she needs to go and catch her train into London. I say I'll stay and do the washing up. I don't want to go outside just yet.

She gives me a hug and looks at me like she wishes she could help. I want to tell her she is helping but I don't know how to say it without getting upset. I feel selfish for being sad when everyone's trying so hard to make it better. I feel like getting back in the bath and resting my face in the water until it's over.

3

At your funeral your dad stood apart from the rest of your family. He'd kept his coat on with his collar turned up, and where it grazed his hairline I'd noticed how his ears were shaped like yours.

I'd only met him a couple of times. There was that first evening – right at the beginning – when we went back to his house, thinking he was on holiday. Your sister was at yours and we were still in the sneaking-round stages so we decided to make use of his empty house. We were making out in his bed and we heard him come in through the door, not on holiday after all. You pulled on a jumper and some pants; we were drunk and you fell over and I laughed at you hopping about. Then we realised my clothes were downstairs and I was trapped. I thought it was a lot funnier than you did but I didn't know your dad then. You went outside to stall for time and I put on a dressing gown, fastening it with the belt from your trousers because I couldn't find the cord. I'd decided there was nothing else for it but to go out and say hello as if there was nothing going on, and in the morning we all laughed about it over breakfast.

I know he made a lot of mistakes with you. I know how angry you were with him: how much you wanted to prove the way to be a man in your family was not something you'd inherited. I know you loved me for not being scared of him, that he'd always been a person who demanded fear, even when you'd been a child looking up to him for love.

I knew all this, but he stood there on his own at your funeral crying into his fist. He looked all scrunched up. I thought, *maybe you wouldn't want me to be scared now either*, so I went and held his hand.

I don't know where your dad is now. I don't know whether to feel guilty about this. There's so much I'm sad about. I miss your mum and Danielle: us helping her bath Alfie, reading him bedtime stories. I don't know if they're still part of my family, or if you're my boyfriend or my ex-boyfriend now. I don't know how I could go and visit them when I feel guilty that you died and I didn't.

4

So I've finished washing up and I've posted Gabriella's keys through the letterbox and I'm outside on the pavement. It's a gorgeous Sunday – even though it's 5 p.m. – and standing outside her house I notice the sunshine for the first time. The light is making the pavement look clean but it's still gruff enough to feel friendly. The debris from last night is scattered on the pavements in patches of sunlight. It's like there are enough wonky bits I can be part of it.

My phone rings and I look down and it's Danny. I haven't seen him since we all went out. I miss him, but I don't know if I can tell him that. I let the phone ring out, watching the screen flash and trying to decide what to do. He calls me straight back, and this time I pick it up.

'Holly? I'm sorry to call like this, but Frank's been taken to hospital.'

I can hear a bird saying something but the sounds feel like they're coming from a long way away.

'Holly? They think he's had a stroke.'

5

It was Sunday 3rd June and I was in bed at a friend's house in Dollis Hill. We had loose plans to get up and go see a bit of the Queen's Diamond Jubilee flotilla but we'd decided not to set an alarm. I'd put on my glasses and switched on my phone. It was 11.03. I had a voicemail. I went to the toilet, got a glass of water because I was feeling pretty rough, and got back into bed to listen.

I expected it to be you, laughing at my sporadic texting the night before, finding my inability to type while drunk funny. I let the T-Mobile lady tell me I had a new message and waited for your voice. It took me a few seconds to recognise your sister's.

She'd called two hours before at 9.08 a.m. She said you'd been hit by a car and taken to the intensive care unit at York Hospital. You were waiting for brain surgery. Her voice told me I needed to get there as quickly as I could.

My fingers were in my mouth now and I was biting them. My friend came into the room and I handed her the phone. I got out of bed and put on my coat over the shorts and vest I'd borrowed from her to sleep in. Then I sat down on the floor and started crying, because the only shoes I had were the ones I'd worn out dancing the night before. They'd given me blisters, and I couldn't wear them to a hospital – they were too high – and I didn't have any jeans or a jumper with me – only my dress and I'd spilt wine on it – and I didn't even know how to get to York from Dollis Hill.

My friend had taken my phone and got the lady on the voice-mail machine to play the message again and she sat down next to me when it had finished and put her arms round me.

I said, 'Is he going to be OK?'

'He's going to be fine,' she replied.

6

I can't concentrate on what Danny is saying. There's an Evian bottle filled with piss – lid on – placed on top of a litter bin about two metres from where I'm standing. I really want to send it streaming, splash it out onto the concrete floor in the sun. I don't think I could get the lid off with just one hand without spilling it on me though and I'm still on the phone. I think about picking it up and shaking it. I really want to feel how warm it is and

I wonder whether – if it's not fresh – the sun has enough heat in it today to have kept it at body temperature. The air does feel hot and I think to myself that maybe it's the start of the summer. It's too early for that really though; it's still only March and it's been raining almost every day but it's a nice thought. I imagine the bottle like a blood-heated thigh in my hand.

I don't say anything and Danny's voice keeps going.

'Holly? Are you there? We're in the hospital. It's OK; he was with Jackie and she called me and we're there now. It looks like it may have only been a TIA so it's more of a scare than anything but I thought you'd want to come down here.'

I don't want to go down there. I feel like I really need to go somewhere but not there, and I start to cry a bit so I ask, 'Where's Harris?'

'We left him with Jackie's neighbour. Holly, are you OK?'

'Danny someone's weed in a water bottle and left in on top of a bin. I don't really know why they'd do that. And what about Gabriella? She's gone wine tasting.'

'I know; we've spoken to her. She's OK; she's going to visit him in the morning. Look, do you want me to come and get you? I've got the car here.'

'It's OK, I'll catch a bus.'

'You want the number 1. I think it goes from the station and it won't take long. Or grab a cab. I can come get you if you want?'

'Is he OK?'

'I think so, yeah. I think he's going to be fine. See you in a bit.'

'Yeah.'

I stand outside Gabriella's house and think about Frank lying in a building full of people who are dying.

I think about corridors and machines and double doors that are pushed open by trollies being rushed from one department to another. I wonder why all hospital entrances have revolving doors.

I reach out for something to steady myself with but I'm standing on the pavement so there isn't really anything there to hold.

7

London was packed for the Jubilee celebrations but the distraction of other people's bodies rammed onto tubes was easier than the quiet empty carriage on the train up to York. I don't remember buying a ticket at King's Cross but I did, and I found my train and I got on it. I sat on one of the seats with a table, facing backwards.

As I'd left her house my friend had pushed a puzzle book into my hand. She'd said I might need something to do on the train. I sat there staring at a crossword. I was dehydrated. The crossword was one of the cryptic ones you hated and I pretended to understand to wind you up but I felt useless because I couldn't do any of the clues. I had a headache and I probably smelt. I tried to google the words your sister had said in her message but my signal kept going in and out. I bought a Snickers from the trolley and looked at it.

8

I can't do it. I can't go to the hospital to see Frank so I turn off my phone and walk back to the house and sit in my room. I think about the time at Borough Market when Frank told me he didn't mind not having children because he hoped his friends saw him as family. I know Danny will have told him I'm coming, and I think about him sitting in a hospital bed waiting. Maybe Frank isn't even conscious; maybe he doesn't realise he's wrapped in clean sheets and attached to a machine that beeps. I leave my room again and go running like a river that needs to find somewhere to be.

The hospital is only a fifteen-minute walk from my house but I've never been that far. I always run the other way, or down along the front. Tonight I turn right and run along the prom towards the West Pier, but I have to stop because I can't see where I'm going. I walk down to the edge of the water, tripping a bit where the stones fall away under my feet and where my tears get in the way of my eyes. I pick up the biggest rock I can find and throw it at the sea. I keep going, picking up stones and throwing them, and I'm crying too much to watch them land but I keep chucking them until I can't stand up anymore.

Frank makes the stones dance when he throws them into the water. He's always been magic. Now he's had a stroke and I don't understand what that means. I sit down and put my head on my knees until the shaking stops. I sit there as it gets darker. I watch the birds dip and wish I could be brave enough to go and find Frank. I wish I could be brave enough to believe in something again: to believe in a love that isn't always awful because it's ending.

9

You can watch car accidents on YouTube. People have made compilations of them: like mix tapes or photo albums. Normally the driver loses control, and then there's a bit of skidding and crumpling metal or branches breaking. If you watch them with the sound turned on you can hear people say things like, 'Watch out!' or 'Oh boy!' If the camera's inside the car the driver normally screams.

The woman who killed you was called Elizabeth Whitworth and she was driving a red Renault Scenic. She hit the brakes but you didn't even look. She says she screamed. She cried a lot too; I heard her, on the statement she gave the police. Your body broke the windscreen. You slid back down it while she tried to stop. Your arm was crushed under the car and your insides all came open. You were unconscious right up until your brain gave in at the hospital and you died. These are all facts. Renault Scenics are big cars and you were just a person.

Elizabeth wrote to me once, after the funeral. She said she has nightmares where she sees your face hitting the windscreen. Loud noises give her panic attacks. She said she knows it wasn't anybody's fault but she'll feel guilty for the rest of her life. She asked me if I was OK for money and signed the letter 'Lizzy'.

I don't know what the difference is between the fear that makes you move and the fear that freezes your bones and holds you still. Maybe you didn't see her at all. But when I think of how scared you must have been I have to hold the top of my head to stop it coming off.

I wrote back and asked her if she watches the videos too. If she sits at night on her own trying to understand how it happened. If she could help me find one that looked like you did so I could stop searching. She didn't reply. I think of her when I don't sleep, knowing she's replaying it all too.

10

Before my driving test Gabriella told me everyone worries about their reaction speed, that it doesn't take losing someone in a car crash to make driving frightening. She told me I just had to change the image of you I saw when I blinked. She said, 'Put a picture of Sam smiling on the dashboard. You've got to get the hospital bed out of your eyes when you look at the road.' She told me death slows down the imagination for a while, gets it stuck on nightmares.

I've learnt to drive, but I can't get up to go and see my friend. I feel selfish and ashamed but I sit on the beach and hope that Frank will forgive me for letting him down. I feel cold and my ears are hot and I'm sick. I go and buy some crisps and a bottle of water. I walk back down to the sea again afterwards and sit with my back against one of the groynes, hidden in the shadow of it. Up to my right the buildings and the streetlamps lining the edge of the town are like bleached white teeth. To the left, the sea is a mouth with its tongue ripped out: wide and dark and only able to choke.

I think about Frank sitting on his roof and drinking tea and him telling me not to worry about anything. I close my eyes and send magic into the sky and hope and hope he'll be OK.

I sit outside all night. It rains twice but I stop feeling cold after a while. I've chosen a bit of the beach where I can disappear into shadow. Sometimes there are voices behind me but I know I'm hidden; whoever they belong to won't see me. I hold my breath until they're gone; I don't want to share the air.

I think about the water washing me away like I'm a pebble. I hope it doesn't, but I'm tired so I curl into a ball. I fall asleep after a bit, sheltered by the pier and the slope of stones behind me.

When the sun rises I feel empty. The sky over the sea felt so expectant but it's just daytime again; nothing's happened. The noise of cars and people is getting thicker, so I get up and start walking. It hurts because I'm cold and my knees and elbows feel shrunken and tight. There's a pain in my chest and I'm struggling to breathe but I go all the way down past Marrocco's.

There's a woman sat outside with a baby, feeding it ice cream with a teaspoon. She looks so calm and serene and I want to shout at her to watch out because anything could go wrong. I start running past the tennis courts and Danny's flat and I keep going. I think about kissing him and try to stop thinking about anything. When I get to Millionaire's Row I turn right and walk around the streets, jogging a bit sometimes, but mostly walking. I have £2.73 left in my pocket so I get some mini cocktail sausages and another bottle of water from a grocery store. I nearly shake the person behind the till but I don't know what to say except *it's dangerous here; be careful* and it comes out as a whisper and I don't think anyone hears me. Then I walk a bit further and I think about looking for the ice cream lady and her baby but they're probably gone so I sit on a bench until it gets dark.

I wonder if the bottle of piss is still there on that bin or if someone has taken it away.

11

The first time I got my period after you died, I lay on my side on the bathroom floor and cried. I held onto my stomach and it hurt. We were always so careful; I don't know if I'd been hoping for an accident or a miracle. I think I just hadn't stopped believing in forever yet; I thought maybe you'd find a way to stay with me. My insides left my body and it felt like losing a child.

I wanted to hold something I loved as much as you. I wanted to see your face in someone else's.

Instead I lay there on the floor and let myself bleed. I'd failed to grow you back inside me. I was completely alone.

12

It's Ellie who finds me. She sits down next to me on the bench and I look up.

She's brought antibiotics and a flask of ginger tea. I don't ask where she got them or how she knew where I was; I just curl into her lap. I've been cold for a long time now and my fingers are stiff, like tiny rolled up newspapers.

'He's going to be OK, Holly,' she says.

I look at her.

'Are they sure?'

She nods. She strokes my hair and asks me why I'm out here on my own.

'I thought it would help me feel nothing,' I say.

'I shouldn't think that's working too well.'

'Not really.'

'For the best I think, in the long run.'

She lights a cigarette and passes it to me.

'Is he still at the hospital?'

'Yeah, but they're letting him go in the morning. It was only a mini stroke so they'll have to monitor him and follow it up but they think he'll be alright.'

There's a silence while I draw on my cigarette but my lungs are itchy and sore so I cough and just sit there with it instead.

'I didn't come.'

'I know. Are you alright?'

She lights a second cigarette for herself and waits.

'I didn't get to Sam in time,' I say. 'I arrived eleven minutes after he'd stopped breathing and he was still warm. I hate hospitals.'

'No one's cross with you Holly.'

'Not even Danny?'

'Danny's worried. You turned off your phone so for all we knew you could have thrown yourself off a cliff or something dramatic like that. We were a bit concerned but we guessed what had happened.'

She puts an arm round me and I breath out as I lean into her.

'But it's OK, sweetheart; you're here. And Frank's going to be fine.'

'What time is it?'

'About 11. You've been on the run for a while.'

'I'm sorry.'

'Don't be, darling. It's all been incredibly exciting. I've never been part of a search party before. But if you're going to disappear again you must dress a little warmer. Personally I think you look great and I can tell why you've gone for the bedraggled look, but Frank will be up in arms. We all love you so much. I hope you know that.'

Later Danny walks down to where we're sitting and tells

me I'm going to stay at Gabriella's for the rest of the night. He doesn't say anything else; he just gives me a scarf and drives me and Ellie up to the London Road. Gabriella gives me pyjamas to wear and cooks lasagne. We sit and eat and neither of them mention that it's the middle of the night.

Harris is at Gabriella's house now too, and he sleeps at the end of my bed. I haven't slept properly in days and when I wake up in Gabriella's spare room there's a little vase of flowers on the table next to me. My parents come down later that day and drive me home.

13

At your funeral the priest said, 'All that any of us are is an accumulation of our moments. Every act we take part in is written on the definition of our lives forever, and nothing good that Sam did will pass away with him. Those moments will remain as residue in the lives of the people who loved him.'

I'd told Frank about this and about how it bothered me because surely that meant our fights – the crap stuff we'd done, the mean things – would always be there too.

He said love didn't work like that.

14

I sit with my mum watching reruns of *Grand Designs*. I curl into her on our sofa and Dad makes big pots of soup that I eat out of a mug. I tell them I'm still really sad and they say they think that's normal. I tell them how scared I am that one day I'll stop missing you. I tell them how scared I am of being happy. They just hug me then, and we sit with it, the pain and the memories, and time passes on the hands of my little watch.

I call your mum that weekend and she tells me she misses me. I ask if I can go and see her over Easter. I tell her I'm sorry I sent your Christmas present to her house, that I hope it didn't upset her and I should have said sorry before but I didn't know how. We both cry and she tells me everything upsets her so I shouldn't worry.

15

I go back to Brighton about a week later. Frank has invited me and Gabriella over for dinner the evening I get back. I take a cake I've baked at Mum and Dad's to give to him. They drive me all the way to his and when we get there they get out of the car to say goodbye and we all cry a bit.

'I'll see you in a week anyway, after Easter,' I say. 'I love you.'

'Call us, OK? And no more staying up all night.'

They drive off and Frank opens the door, smiling. He looks a bit tired and is moving slower than normal but he's wearing a lop-sided party hat and music's blaring out of his speakers. The house is filled with the smell of steak and fried onions.

'Gabby couldn't resist the opportunity to cook for me. Who knew an escape from hospital was such a good excuse for a party. And you've brought cake!'

We go through to the kitchen where Gabriella is stood at the hob, sleeves rolled up and flicking onions round a frying pan. She winks at me and throws over a party hat. I notice that an armchair's been moved in from the sitting room. Frank stands next to it, one hand leaning slightly on its back.

'It's a sorry cake really,' I say. 'For standing you up at the hospital.'

'Holly,' he replies. 'I completely understand. Hospitals are dreadful places and a terrible choice for a date. The cake more than makes up for it and thank God for all your baking lessons because it looks quite edible.'

I put on the hat and he carries on, 'If I'd actually been dying it would have been inexcusable of course. When the time comes for that I need you to be ready to sing at my bedside. But I don't intend to die for a good few years yet and when I do we won't rely on public transport to get you there.'

Gabriella laughs.

'I mean it though,' I say. 'I really wanted to come; I just –'

Frank looks at me seriously and I remember he's a magician. He smiles.

'Enough said. You're here now. Get yourself a drink. What kind of a party do you think this is?'

Gabriella serves up the steak, and I sit down next to them with a bottle of beer. Frank taps it on the bottom and the cap pops off.

'Now,' he says, 'let's quiz Gabriella on her romantic exploits from the other week; don't think I've forgotten in all the drama that you've been off gallivanting with handsome strangers.'

16

Danny rings me at lunch the next day. I've been hoping he'd call but I haven't known what I wanted to say. *I'm running away from*

so many things; please don't take it personally. Can I just have a bit of
time to work out how you're tied up in all this?

'I heard you were back. Are you sticking around for Easter or going back home?'

The question surprises me. We've barely spoken since we kissed on the beach and I don't know how to answer him; I'm going to York to visit your family but that feels complicated so I say, 'I'm going away for the weekend. Why?'

'I want to see you before you go. I've got you an Easter egg.'

'OK . . . I'm teaching tonight, but after? Or we could have breakfast before work tomorrow.'

'Come over later,' he says.

I do. He buzzes me up to his flat. The floor of the lift is green; this feels incongruous. When I get to the seventh floor the lift pings like it's a microwave and I've just finished cooking.

I walk down the corridor to Danny's door and he's left it open for me so I go straight inside. He's sat in the living room at the dining table reading a book. He buzzed me in about two minutes earlier so he's either deeply engrossed or he's acting.

'Hey, Danny.'

17

I get the train from Brighton to Victoria, then the tube to King's Cross and the train to York. I sleep for a lot of the journey, and the bits I'm awake for are sore.

At York your mum meets me at the station. Your eyes look out at me from her face. I swallow a bit. She hugs me for a little too long as other people come through the ticket barrier and go off to wherever they're going. She says, 'Don't stay away so long next time,' and we make our way into the city centre to walk by the river and remember things. We speak in English and French, understanding each other but not always being able to say what we mean. It's like it's always been; the words aren't the bits that matter.

We meet Danielle and Alfie in town and I watch him feed the ducks. I go and squat down next to him and he says, 'Uncle Sam couldn't come with you today because he's in heaven now. Mummy says you might be feeling sad. Are you feeling sad?'

'I am a bit, Alfie, but it's good to see you.'

'It's good to see you too. Did you bring me an Easter egg?'

I laugh.

'Yeah I did. You can have it in the morning.'

He smiles at me and offers me a slice of bread. I take it and break off a chunk to throw to the ducks.

We go to church on Easter Sunday and your mum cries as the priest reads the bit from the gospel about Jesus rising again. Danielle holds her hand and we all sing that song about the Lord of the Dance and when we go home we put on Ray Charles and dance in the kitchen while we prepare roast vegetables together and the beef cooks. Your mum doesn't want to let me help. I just about get away with peeling some potatoes and then I play with Alfie while they finish up. We eat round a big oak table in the living room. It's new since the funeral and the house feels more settled into now.

Your mum says she wants to have a party on your birthday in the autumn: somewhere in London so all your friends can get together.

'Are you in touch with many of them?' I ask.

'They write on big days,' she says. 'Occasionally some of them phone. But it's hard when the only reason to talk is feeling sad.'

'Everyone asks after to you, Holly,' Danielle says. She's gentle, softer than you but as direct. 'I think they found it pretty hard to lose both of you.'

I nod. Being with your family is taking me back to all our old grooves: the people we slid along with. I've pushed myself so far away from them all.

'She's here now,' your mum says.

When we've put Alfie to bed we stay up late into the night talking about you, drinking wine and then whisky, and it isn't as sad as I thought it would be. It's like finding old clothes you've forgotten about, and even though they're slightly patchy they fit so well. It's so good to be with people who remember you and I feel bad for having been so far away.

Your mum says she has a box of your things she's kept for me to look through before I go home. She says there are a bunch of cards and letters I'd sent you there too and she hadn't wanted to throw them away. I feel a bit embarrassed because I know some of the stuff I've written in them is a bit fruity. She must know what I'm thinking about because she laughs and says she thinks we were lovely. *Nous sommes seulement dans le passé. Je suis moi maintenant; je ne sera jamais nous.*

Your mum goes to bed but your sister sits up with me a bit longer and we make a cup of tea and sing along to the music a bit and talk about stuff going on in the world. I tell her she reminds me of you a lot and she says she doesn't know how to make your mum happy. We sit on the sofa and try to fill the spaces in each other for a while.

Just before we go to bed we rinse out the tea cups in the kitchen and she says, 'I'm sure you know this anyway, Holly, but when you fall in love again it will be alright with us. It would've been alright with Sam too.'

18

I haven't spoken to Danny since I left his house the morning after I'd felt like I was being cooked in his microwave lift. We'd slept in his bed together, with all our clothes on and our mouths pushed together and his left hand holding mine on the pillow and his right hand where my hips start to curve around. We talked about none of it and I left before breakfast feeling guilty that someone other than you felt so comfortable.

19

In that last April I'd gone away on holiday with my friends from school for a week and I'd promised you a postcard. Instead I'd written you seven little letters: one each day. You'd kept them all in a box with other bits and pieces, some of which I can't place at all. There's a ticket stub from *Avatar*, which we'd been to see together; that token we'd won in an arcade in Scarborough; a little menu from our friend Ruby's twenty-first birthday party; and a couple of pebbles and a Christmas cracker hat. I don't know why you kept those.

We always told each other not to bother with cards on Valentine's Day because we agreed we didn't need a designated day for being nice to each other. But one day in the summer I'd given you a 'This Is Not a Valentine's Day Card' and we'd gone out for cocktails and to one of those old-fashioned cinemas with red velvet seats.

You told me once you loved listening to me singing in the shower and I'd been embarrassed because in my head the bathroom was soundproof. But you'd said you liked to hear my voice bounce through the walls and to think about me in there naked. You'd said you could never hear the words because of the water and the concrete, but you liked to imagine I was singing love songs to you. I'd laughed at you and told you you were soppy, but in your 'This Is a Not Valentine's Day Card' I'd written: *All my songs are for you, Sam.*

I find that card in your box, sat on the same bed where I'd sat and smelt for you on the day of your funeral. The room is too hot because your mum always keeps the heating on and I'm wearing Frank's jumper and it's making me itch. I bite into my cheeks. I can't stay sitting down with all these things you've stashed away so instead I get up and walk around the room. I'm angry with the stupid rose-patterned wallpaper, angry with you. I don't feel like my skin can take any more tears without coming off altogether and I'm not going to cry. I don't want to blow my nose anymore. I feel like my face is raw from it all, like your body on the road, like your head in my eyes when I close them, like every time I dream of skin and faces and traffic.

20

Ellie phones me in the morning.

'How's York, Holly?'

'It's OK.'

'Do you mean intensely painful and overwhelming?'

I laugh.

'A bit. It's good to be here though.'

'Sweetheart, there is nothing bitty about total and utter despair. Danny told me you two snogged. Are you very confused?'

'Yeah, kind of. Are you annoyed with me?'

'Goodness no. Mr DeVito is devilishly attractive; it was inevitable at some point. I just wanted to check you're OK.'

'I'm alright. Just riding it out, you know? Thanks for phoning, Ellie. You're great.'

'I know. Listen, Frank once told me – on a very thin day – that whenever I felt frightened by the pain I should close my eyes and count to ten and then keep crying until something was funny again. He told me to remember babies learn to laugh before they learn to speak, and because happiness is as instinctive as pain, I'd never be completely without both. Now as a doctor of neuroscience I can tell you this isn't entirely true and the total physical devastation you're currently experiencing is totally valid. But at least Frank's a cheesy old optimist eh?'

I laugh at her.

'Are you in pain, Ellie?' I say.

She thinks.

'I'm always very cold, but it's getting better. Don't worry about me; just hurry home, OK? We can nuzzle each other into full recovery.'

21

I call a taxi and say goodbye to your mum and Danielle and Alfie at the house. We hug and cry; that seems to be what happens when I say goodbye to people now. But they're good tears, and I feel like we've all breathed something out in the night.

I ask the taxi to take me to York Hospital. When we get there I go in through the revolving doors and stand just inside the waiting room. I must look upset because a woman walks past me and asks if I'm OK.

I say, 'Yeah I am, thanks. I just don't like hospitals.'

She smiles and says, 'I don't think anyone does.'

The things I remember about the hospital are the vending machine in the waiting room by the entrance, the green pot plant outside the Intensive Care Unit and the revolving doors. They are all still here. I walk through the same corridors with the strip lighting overhead and think about the person whose job it is to water the plants. There is a little bug in the corner of the wall outside the ICU and the harshness of the light makes it pop in my eyes, like a camera flash staining my lids when I close them. I stand there and look at the pot plant, and nobody dies.

Afterwards I walk outside and stand – leaning on the hospital wall. I haven't noticed that I'm hot until I feel the air on my face and ears, and I stand there, leaning backwards and breathing. I light a cigarette and watch a taxi pull up and a woman on crutches carrying a carrier bag with the hospital's name printed on it gets in. It drives off and I look at the sky. It's unremarkable. I unclench my fist and put my lighter back into my pocket.

There's a couple sitting on a bench not far from where I'm standing. She's pregnant and he's smoking and they look like they're teenagers or maybe in their early twenties. I watch as she puts her hand to her stomach and then pulls his in, and they look back up at each other and laugh as their baby moves. He kisses her and she wrinkles her nose and says something about the smoke. He throws his cigarette on the floor and treads it out, and then puts his head in his hands with his elbows resting on his knees and his ear by her stomach. It looks like maybe he's saying something to her bump. She puts one of her hands on his back and he looks up at her sideways. He says something else and she laughs again and gives him a shove. I wonder what they're going to call their baby and then I look away at something else – a car driving, a door slamming – and when I look back at the bench they're gone. It still hurts. I think maybe it always will.

22

We explored each other for almost five years. We opened up all the bits of each other we were too scared to show anyone else. I climbed into your mouth and listened to you whisper. We held each other out and decided the space between us was only there so we could make it disappear. You let me fly in your arms and I let you hold me. You were in every dream I had about the future; all the things my body can do were meant to be with you. I don't know how we go back to the beginning and start that again with someone else. I don't know how to split myself open for another person when all they'll be able to see is that I'm broken and grieving.

Danny has texted me but I haven't opened the message yet. I don't know if I'm ready to try.

23

I look around for the bus stop but I can't find it so I ask someone in pale-green overalls who's standing near me where it is. They point it out and I go and wait. As the bus to York station pulls away and I start my journey back to London, I text Frank: *Back on the bike. Should you need me to sing at your bedside anytime soon I'm available. Other locations preferred but hospitals tolerated.*

He replied: *Super news. Feeling much better this end. Come back soon. Harris misses you.*

24

My brother was born early. He'd had to live in an incubator for four weeks and when Mum was pregnant with me she'd told my dad she wasn't going to let me out unless they'd be able to take me home straight away. I was born on the exact day I was due and I came out with hiccups. Rob had been told he was going to have a new brother or sister and that when I was born he'd be allowed to choose which way round my first name and middle name went. When he came to visit me in the hospital just after I was born, he told Mum and Dad I should be allowed an extra name for being on time. They'd asked him what he thought it should be and he'd said Holly, and they'd decided they liked that more than Jennie or Emma so they'd called me that.

When we were little Mum and Dad used to take us to Brighton on day trips and we'd walk along the prom from Marrocco's cafe to the pier and back. Rob would bring a clipboard and a pen and we'd walk ahead of them, weaving in and out of the beach huts. It was always a bit of a squeeze getting in between them, which made us feel adventurous, and Rob would describe each one to me in detail as we went, writing down my comments on a bit of paper tucked into the clipboard. When we got to the end of the row I would decide which of the beach huts I wanted to live in; we'd consult our notes, shake hands and the game would be done.

When I turned sixteen, Rob had told me the only thing he needed to teach me as my wise older brother was that when I got drunk I should take two paracetamol, eat two slices of bread and drink two pints of water before I went to bed. He said if I did that I'd never have a hangover.

The first time I got really smashed he was home on holiday from his first year at university. I'd been out at a party and I'd got home alright but when I was in our hall I phoned him in his room asking him to come down and help me. He got me up the stairs and into my bed and went and found me water, bread and painkillers.

In the morning I went into his room a bit worse for wear and we sat in his bed watching *Neighbours*, him laughing at me for being able to make it home but not being able to get myself up the stairs.

When Rob and his girlfriend got a place together I imagined them doing the beach-hut thing, following estate agents around flats and making notes on a clipboard. I'd told Rob on Skype and he'd laughed at me.

When they'd moved in I was in my last year at university and he'd used the laptop to show me round. I'd felt weird about how grown-up he'd got but then the next day he'd texted me because he couldn't remember how to make macaroni cheese.

25

I sleep on the train back to London and dream of red ants growing on trees instead of blossom. At King's Cross I take the tube back to Victoria where I meet Mum and Dad for dinner. They give me an Easter egg and a hug.

'How was the trip, Hols?'

'Weird. Good weird, I guess. Made me miss a whole load of people I haven't seen in a while.'

'We missed you too.'

'It's only been a week, Mum!' I laugh at her but I take her arm as we walk around the corner and give it a squeeze. I know she's worried about me disappearing again. I am too, but I feel like I'm here at the minute.

We cross the road past *Wicked* and *Billy Elliot*. Dad tells me Rob's coming to meet us too; he's got some news he wants to tell me in person.

It's raining but only a bit. The edges of the road are filled with grey sludge where the wheels of buses and bikes have ground the city's muck into rainwater. It creeps up round the edges of my brown boots and I wish I was wearing something colourful.

Rob arrives at the restaurant just after we've got to our table and we all get up to say hi.

'Happy Easter, Rob.'

'Yeah, you too. How you doing?'

We sit down and I look at them.

'So, what's the big news? These two said you had something exciting to tell me.'

He looks at Dad who sort of shrugs his shoulders and smiles. Rob fiddles with his napkin and looks back at me. He's smiling but his fingers rub together through the white material.

'Well,' he says, 'I'm getting married. I asked Lucy yesterday and she said yes.'

'What? That's amazing!'

We all start laughing and I jump up to hug him and knock over a vase on our table.

'Where is she? Why didn't she come?'

'I wanted to tell you by myself. I knew you'd be pleased but I just thought . . . She's coming in a bit though, if that's OK.'

'Yeah of course! Rob, this is so exciting.'

We sit down again and me and Mum try to stand the flower up at the same time so we both knock it back over, which sets us all off again.

When we stop laughing Rob looks at me a bit funny and goes to say something. I know what he means and I say, 'Don't. I'm pleased. I'm so pleased. It's my favourite thing that's happened all year. Maybe ever.'

I am happy, just not as much as I want to be. I feel a bit dull and tired, but he's smiling so much I smile back. Dad orders prosecco and when Lucy gets there we do it again: the hugging and the laughing. She sits next to me and we order pasta; it comes and we eat it. There's a CD of an Italian folk band playing in the background and the waiter tells us that they sell it for a fiver. I buy a copy and give it to Rob and Lucy with the flower from the vase. As we leave she asks me if I'll be her bridesmaid and we hug and laugh again. Everyone else looks so shiny and I don't want them to notice I'm fading away.

Later that night I get the train back to Brighton. I walk home from the station holding my Easter egg. The wind smells of spring and the moist air above the sea is full of stars, posted there like thoughts.

I'm happy for my brother, but the idea of love that lasts forever hangs in the air around me. It blocks up my throat like offal.

26

That Wednesday I have plans to go round Frank's house to learn how to make a Swiss roll. When I get there he tells me he doesn't feel like cooking and asks if I want to go to the greyhound races instead. We drive over to the stadium in Hove leaving Harris at home, and walk down to the track to sit and look at the line-up.

Frank looks better but a bit older round the edges of his eyes. It surprises me when I say I'm hungry and there's a bag of toffees already in my pocket.

'Does your magic extend to predicting the outcome of greyhound races?' I say.

'Oh no, magic has no capacity to help me cheat.'

I laugh at him because I've watched him play cards so I know this isn't true. He gives me a little wink and nicks a toffee. I notice his shoelace is undone and I tell him. He looks down and shakes his foot for a bit. When he puts it down again the laces are re-tied.

'You're incredible.'

Frank's policy is to bet £1 on every race on the dog with the best name. We stand by the finish line and shout encouragement, going completely berserk when – in the third race – our dog comes second and we nearly win £1.50.

In the last race of the day we put £5 on Brute McGee with odds of 25:1.

'Brute McGee sounds like a winning name; we can't go wrong with that.'

'If Brute comes first we'll win £130, Frank. This may be a sign we have in fact gone wrong.'

We laugh and stand there waiting for the starting gun. Brute starts slowly but in the second half of the lap he accelerates and begins closing in on the dogs at the front. Frank and I look at each other and start yelling. We watch as Brute finishes neck and neck with the dog who's been ahead. It's a photo finish and Brute just loses out.

We pick up a curry on our way home and sit in Frank's kitchen together eating it and reflecting on the fortune we very nearly made.

'What are you up to tonight, Holly? Out on the razzle?

'It's quiz night.'

'Of course! A second chance in one day to make your fortune.'

I need to have a shower after the races so I arrive late to the quiz. I can see on the scoreboard that our team are doing well. It looks like we're in about third or fourth place, and I arrive just as the picture round's being handed out. I see them in the corner of the room and walk over. Ellie and Mira are sitting round one side of the table, immersed in their conversation and not really paying attention.

As I arrive at the table they look up and Ellie asks, 'Do you have a contract on the room that you stay in? How long have you paid to be there for?'

'I don't know,' I reply. 'I think I just have to give a month's notice. It's all pretty casual because it's basically just a room in the loft. Why?'

'It turns out my housemates were shagging and now they've broken up and want to move out,' Mira says. 'One of them's going to London and the other one says she doesn't want to stay anywhere he used to live. It's a bit of a joke to be honest but I was wondering if you two might want to move in.'

'I was just saying I wasn't sure if you'd want to because I didn't know how much longer you were planning to stay down here,' Ellie says. 'But if you do, I think it'd be great.'

'Oh my God, yeah – I mean we'd have to talk about rent and stuff – but that'd be amazing.'

Sean pours a glass of wine and pushes it towards me, pulling out a seat for me to sit down.

'Holly, now you're finally here perhaps you could persuade these two to stop nattering and help us answer some of these questions.'

We all laugh and Ellie and Mira turn to the pictures but I stay standing. I haven't seen Danny since the night before I'd gone to York and I've been avoiding all of his messages. He doesn't make eye contact with me so I put a hand on his shoulder.

'I'm just going to have a cigarette first actually. Danny, will you come with me?'

Danny doesn't smoke so the others keep looking at the pictures and pretend it's a normal request. I don't know if Danny's told anyone other than Ellie what happened but I imagine they have a fair idea of what's gone on. He stands up and raises his eyebrows at me. I can tell he's annoyed I've been so obvious but he can't say no without making a scene. I turn around and walk out and he follows me onto the street. We stand there while I light up and I shuffle about a bit with my feet, pretending to need to get warm.

27

J'ai peur que tu disparaisses comme un souffle dans l'air. Je ne veux pas que tu sois triste. Je ne peux pas toujours porter cette culpabilité, comme de mauvaises herbes enchevêtrées autour de mes poignets qui m'immobilisent par terre.

28

'Ellie said you went to the dogs,' Danny says.

'Yeah.'

'Did you win anything?'

'No. Nearly though.'

'Right.'

I chew on my bottom lip and am aware of a burn on the tip of my tongue. I wonder where it came from and think it must have been from dinner. It's been a while since I held heat in my mouth until it blistered. After a pause Danny says, 'Margaret Thatcher died today.'

'Yeah, I saw on the news. That's not really what I wanted to talk about though.'

He doesn't say anything so I stall. 'How was your day?'

'It was alright. I went to work. We have a big party coming up at the label so I was just doing some prep for that really. Flyers and things.'

'Cool.'

'It was fine.'

An aeroplane flies overhead and a couple walk out of the pub arguing. They retreat down the road and she swings her handbag at him, narrowly missing his head. As they move in and out of the light cast by successive street lamps their fight is lit up in short bursts, their silhouettes splayed like shadow puppets. I look at Danny but he doesn't seem to find it funny or even really notice, and I can feel my stomach go around faster.

'Look, Danny –'

He turns to face me and I can't think of what to say. I notice that his upper lip has a little cut on it from where he must have nicked himself shaving. I try again.

'I wanted to say sorry about everything these last couple of weeks. It's just –'

I let out a little bit of air: I'm talking without breathing out. 'I feel weird that I haven't seen you.'

He looks blank, using his eyes to look past me or something.

'We don't have to talk about it, Holly; everything's fine. I just got the wrong end of the stick. We were spending a lot of time together and then that night when we kissed and you stayed; I thought you liked me. I guess I was just being stupid or something –'

'You weren't being stupid, I do like you. It's just I went to stay with Sam's family the next day and it was the first time I'd seen them and I'm confused. And then I didn't reply to your messages and I haven't seen you and now I just feel like it's got weird and I really didn't want that to happen.'

I tug at the bottom of my coat, pulling on the zip.

'But what do you want, Holly? I don't think you really know and it makes things pretty difficult for me.'

29

Tu es le cerf-volant maintenant qui s'enfuit dans le vent comme un souffle dans l'air. Je ne sais pas comment rester par terre accrochée à toi, j'essaie de ne pas te lâcher. Nous nous évanouissons.

30

I know that Danny isn't angry but it feels like this is a conversation he's been trying to avoid having with me for a long time. He looks at me like *now we're having it and I'm right because you don't know what you want to say*, and I want to say I'm sorry but I also want to kiss him and I'm finding that really confusing.

He says, 'Let's just go back in and do the quiz, shall we?'

And I say, 'Yeah, I guess so.'

But neither of us goes back inside and I look at him and he takes a step towards me and puts his hands on my shoulders and I lift up my face and sort of squint at him. We stand like that for a while and we both kind of frown at each other and he looks like he's waiting for something. I close my eyes and he kisses me. It goes on for a while, slightly fiercer than the last time but then he takes my hand and it's gentle again. He is so still and I want to climb inside that and rest with him.

We don't say anything else; we just go back inside. We come second in the quiz to the team who have their own T-shirts. They beat us by three points.

31

On Sunday Gabriella tells me Frank has missed his first follow-up appointment with the doctor. He'd told her he was fine and that there was no need for him to go back. She'd made him book another slot and was planning on going with him.

I'm sitting with him one evening, eating apple crumble, when he turns to me and says, 'Not sure I trust doctors. What do you reckon?'

I think about it.

'I think probably best to, yeah.'

He nods and offers me a jug of cream.

'You're probably right. But I'm not as young as you are so – for me – doctors pose a slight threat. They might decide to tell me I'm dying.'

I look at him.

'You're not dying, Frank.'

'No, you're quite right. Let's just hope the doctors are as sensible as you, eh? Don't you want some cream?'

'I'm more of a custard kind of girl.'

He nods and moves his hand over the jug and the sauce goes yellow. I shake my head at him in disbelief.

'If the doctors can't keep you going then the rest of us have no chance at all.'

I pour the custard over my crumble and keep eating.

32

I'm due to move in with Mira and Ellie in mid-May, but I'm worried about money because I know the summer holiday will mean less work. I flick through the newspapers, circling adverts for childcare or cleaning agencies. I register with a couple of recruitment agencies too. They ask me what I'm looking for, and I say I don't really know. I tell them I want to stay in Brighton and would try most things.

I do want to stay. This feels strange when there are so many things I miss. I talk to Frank about it at the book club. He says, 'I asked a taxi driver to take me home once. He asked, "Where's home?" and I told him it's a person, not a place; anyone who tells you otherwise is lying. I gave him my address and said that home was waiting for me there.'

'I'm a nomad,' I say.

'You have some beautiful options,' he replies. 'Love won't always feel so far away.'

Noel tells me they're looking for a youth-outreach officer at Kew Gardens and I should apply. I send the application off that weekend but I don't even get an interview.

I don't really know much about plants so I'm not that surprised. I know what it feels like to grow though, how it feels to dig out weeds and look for the sun.

After the meeting Danny walks me home. We kiss a bit in the porch of the church next to my house. I'm scared to ask him inside. I don't know how to deal with wanting Danny at the same time as I want you.

I kiss you both at the same time. I feel ashamed and scared because I want something I can't have and something I can.

33

The girl who brought the bracelet back from Barbados for me has a beautiful piano. She plays well and I enjoy teaching her, but something about the damp drying in the air makes my fingers itch and I ask her mum if – after our lessons – I can stay and play by myself for a while. She says yes and so Louisa sits on the sofa with a lemonade and I play, stretching the notes out under my fingers and feeling the music in the air around me.

I get into the habit of popping in to Frank's most days before bed and on days when I go round after playing the piano I arrive with my head full of music. Frank and I sit and listen to records instead of talking – his knitting needles clicking in their own rhythms – and I sing along.

One Friday night, after I've been playing at Louisa's, Frank tells me he thinks music is a bit like the sea; it gets inside you and washes out some of the stuff you don't want there.

'I feel like it keeps in some of the stuff you don't want to lose too.'

Frank looks at me for a few seconds.

'It's just working out the difference between the two, isn't it?'

Afterwards I cycle to Danny's house. He's ordered take-away curry, and we eat it on his balcony. I have matar paneer and Peshwari naan and he eats chicken jalfrezi with chapati. I'm glad it's not Chinese, and the view of the sea is so different from the rooftops outside your flat but I can't help thinking about that night you bought a piece of London and we sat and pretended to fly on your balcony.

Danny makes me laugh. He is witty in an easy kind of way and he teases me about how much I love to hear the sea breathe. The little street lights along the front start to glow before it's completely dark and everything hums in an orange in-between time. I'm sorry, Sam, but I don't want to be thinking about you.

It starts to get cold so we leave all the plates and boxes outside and come in. The table in his living room is covered in sketches; he's brought some work home for the weekend. I haven't seen his artwork before and I trace over an ink sketch of a child playing in a stream with my finger. I'm surprised by how much movement there is in the image, and it makes me think of the little kids who run down the beach at the week-end, amazed by the sea, with tiny arms flailing around to keep them balanced as they charge into the water.

'Do you like it?' he asks.

I nod, and he puts his hands against mine, pushing his fingers between my fingers so they interlock. I'm aware of the curry taste in my mouth still and think about cleaning my teeth but he's already kissing me so I fold into him and let his tongue find mine. He takes off my clothes but I don't want to be naked on my own so I take off his too. I'm sitting on the table and he's standing in front of me and I wrap my legs around him. He picks me up and carries me into his bedroom.

'Come under the covers, it's cold.'

He puts me onto the bed and I get under the duvet and he lies down next to me.

'Are you OK?'

'Yeah, I think so.'

'We don't have to do anything.'

I nod.

'I know; I'm OK.'

He smiles at me but I'm finding it difficult to look at him. He moves in next to me and kisses me and I kiss him back. I don't know what I want but it's easier to close my eyes and breathe into it than to try and work out what I'm feeling. We kiss some more and I pull him on top of me.

'Holly, I should get a condom.'

'Yeah, OK.'

He gets one out of the drawer by his bed and he puts it on while he kind of straddles me. I want him to get it on so I can pull him in closer, have him lean down on me like a blanket. I'm cold just lying there, watching him. When he's done he puts the packet on the floor and moves his body in close and pushes into me. I hold him there. We go slow and he looks at me but that's too much so I pull him in so his face is over my shoulder and we're flat to each other. He starts to move faster and I don't want it to stop but I think I'm going to cry so I let my breathing get louder and pretend to come. He finishes just afterwards and I don't want him to move away. I pull him close and we lay tucked up in each other until I'm asleep.

In the morning the others come over with breakfast but it's a blue day so we pack up plates and mugs and flasks of coffee and take it down to the sea with the guitar and a bunch of books. We stay there all day and the sky stays bright. I feel shaky and tearful but I don't really know why. We swim and sing and sit curled up in each other like none of us have ever felt sad. Around lunchtime I walk up to get a coffee from the cafe with Mira and Ellie, who holds my hand.

'Are you OK, poppet? You're quite quiet today.'

I look at them and I don't know what to say. I just start to cry and they stand there and hold me while I shake it all out.

'I'm sorry,' I say. 'I'm fine; I don't know what's wrong with me.'

'Never apologise for feeling things, darling,' says Ellie.

'It means you're still alive,' Mira says. Then she looks at me, 'Bad choice of words?'

I shake my head and smile at her.

'Thanks, Mira, I'm alright.'

She shrugs.

'You don't have to be.'

We get the coffee and walk back to the others. After a bit Ellie says she's cold so we go back to Danny's and drink beer and then tequila, and Sean has some pills so we take them too and then we get a cab into town to go dancing and at some point my brain forgets to remember what's happening. I go home to mine that night and I'm there with Danny again. I'm high and soft and all I want is to squish into him so we kiss and fuck and I don't feel sad at all. Then it's Sunday morning so I get up and go for a run and while my body's moving fast I stop trying to work it all out.

Later when Danny's gone and I pick up my pen to write a song I start to think about you again. I don't want to sing then; I sit in the shower instead and think about this time last year, and about how you'd feel if you knew I was wrapped up in someone else.

Summer

The sea keeps moving.
I am driftwood: sat washed up,
holding myself still.

1

Before I leave the little room in Kemptown I sit and use Copydex to push the wallpaper back together. I'll miss my view of the sea. When I unpack again I put your jumper away in a box under the bed. It's getting worn out and the nights aren't so cold anymore. I change my mind when I go to sleep though and get it back out.

My new room is bigger and I want to stick photos on the wall to make it feel full. But all my pictures have you in. I'm trying to leave you behind.

All this moving makes me feel like I haven't gone anywhere at all. This is not your town but you're mine and we're still here. I'm a tug of war without any fighting; I can't pull away. Danny's coming for dinner and I don't know if I can put your face on the wall.

2

I put lots of stuff in storage when I left for Brighton. Before moving in with Ellie and Mira I shifted it to Mum and Dad's and then into the new place. When I went to get the last batch Danny came with me to help. I put my guitar in the boot and it felt good to be bringing it back to Brighton with me. After the car was packed we all sat around the dining table drinking tea before he and I drove back to the coast. I told Mum and Dad about the job I didn't get at Kew Gardens. They said to keep my eye out for similar things and to keep trying.

Later Rob rang the house and we put him on speaker phone. He told us they'd picked a date for the wedding and would be getting married in January. He asked me if I'd come and stay for a weekend over the summer to help Lucy with some of the dress-type stuff and I said I would. Danny looked at me across the table and smiled, and I smiled back and thought about you.

On the way home we stopped off for petrol and Danny came back to the car with bags full of shopping.

'What's all this?'

'A surprise. Mind your own business, Hollywood.'

I sit in the car with my feet on the dashboard and my chair flipped right back. Danny drums along to the music on the steering wheel. The sun's going down and he looks good in the dusky light. I lean over and give his hand a little kiss on the gear stick. He looks at me and laughs.

'What?'

'Nothing, you're just nice.'

He smiles and I smile back.

That night he cooks dinner for Ellie and Mira and me with the ingredients he's picked up at the garage. He makes a terrible risotto that somehow manages to be burnt and undercooked at the same time.

We laugh about it and get pissed, the four of us, drinking cheap vodka with tonic and lime, and filling the kitchen with reggae and smoke and dancing. At one point Ellie persuades Danny to draw caricatures of the three us and we tape them to the fridge. He's pissed so they're kind of wonky and we laugh as we struggle with the Sellotape.

In the morning we sleep wrapped up in each other for hours, our mouths like attics: musty with smoke and snatches of memories from the night before.

3

Sometimes – when we'd had a fight – you'd go and get your toothbrush and come and find me. You'd dance around, stretching your face out, mouth full of toothpaste, until you made me laugh. I'd stop being angry and you'd kiss me and get toothpaste all on my face, and I'd tell you that you were disgusting.

Mira cleans her teeth while she's sat on the loo. The next morning, she leaves the door open and blows a raspberry at me when I walk past. She sprays toothpaste all over her thighs.

'You're disgusting,' I say, and we laugh.

4

Gabriella went out with her doctor again a few days after the wine tasting and they've started to see each other a lot. He has a young daughter called Cora and one weekend at the end of April I go round on the Sunday and find them sitting in her kitchen. Cora's bent over a bowl of dough and Gabriella's showing her how to knead it.

'You're Holly.'

'It's Talin, right? Nice to meet you.'

I sit opposite him on a wooden stool and watch Gabriella show Cora what to do. Cora laughs as flour springs up in her face. Talin has an easy smile and he watches his daughter lazily as he asks me about teaching and home and what I think about *Purple Hibiscus*, which we're reading for the book club.

Once the bread's in the oven, Cora comes and sits on my lap and tells me she's going to meet a magician later. I tell her she's very lucky and she says she already knows.

'Have you met him?' she asks.

'I have,' I say. 'He rescued me once, by the sea.'

'Were you drowning?'

'Kind of. Although it was more like I'd forgotten how to fly.'

She looks at me with big eyes.

'Are you magic too?'

'No,' I say, 'but Frank's quite good at making you feel that way. You better watch out for things that just appear in your hands. He's very clever like that.'

As I go to leave later on Gabriella follows me out into the hall.

'What do you think?' she says.

'He's lovely; I definitely approve.'

She gives me a hug.

'Have fun with Frank.'

I walk away feeling a bit left behind. I sit on the curve of the marina wall and watch the waves. Sadness comes at me from nowhere sometimes. I don't mind; it feels like part of me is lost without it. When I'm sad, I know you were real. When Danny calls I ignore it. I turn off my phone and watch the waves. I'm scared of hurting him but I need to go slowly, like the water does when the last bits of a wave are slipping back down the beach and into the sea.

5

We plan a big house-warming for June and send invites to all our friends from school and university. I put letters inside mine, memories and apologies, and texts start to trickle in from the different spots of home I have. Things are changing. I have a house in Brighton where I unpack and stretch out. My old friends anchor me and I start to feel like I'm climbing in the sky again. But I'm in between things, living in gaps, still trying to find somewhere to rest for a while that feels like it fits. It's like there's a tightrope stretched and shaking inside me and I don't know who or what to balance on it. I watch the people at the West Pier trying to walk on the rope between the poles and sometimes they fall. Maybe that's all that balancing is: the bits in between collapse.

6

Danny and I go cycling at the weekend. I strap my guitar to the back of my bike and he laughs at me. We go east along the coast and stop for a picnic at the top of the cliffs. We sit for a while, him drawing, me writing a song. The sea is all frothy and rhythmic and after a while I put my guitar down and doze for a bit, my head in his lap and my eyes on the water. That evening we play chess at the St James again and I win in six moves. He pretends to be outraged and I laugh at him.

'Playing you is no fun; it's way too easy.'

'I don't understand it, you seem so nice but give you a chessboard and you're a ruthless serial killer.'

'That's kind of the point, DeVito.'

It's a beautiful evening so we leave the pub and walk down to the front. We buy doughnuts at the entrance to the pier and I really want to go on a rollercoaster so we wander down through the arcades to where the rides are. We get tokens from the guy in the kiosk and get in the queue.

During the ride Danny shouts at me over the noise and the whirling.

'You're really sexy upside down.'

I look across at him and he laughs.

7

I still have the card you gave me for my birthday last May. It's in the bottom drawer of my desk underneath a bunch of other bits and pieces, pretending it was put there by accident.

It was the kind of day where London swells in heat. We decided at the last minute to cancel the reservation we'd made for lunch and we spent the day by the canal in Angel. We went to a supermarket and you bought a birthday picnic: bottles of lager, avocados, mozzarella, salt-and-vinegar Chipsticks, raspberries and those Dutch circular waffles with syrup in the middle of them. We sat on the bit of the towpath that sticks out into a kind of veranda on the stretch between Angel and Hoxton and scooped the avocado out of its skin with our fingers. We laid down and swigged beer and talked about nothing, smiling in the sunshine, and our friends trickled down to meet us, bringing music and blankets.

I sat between your legs, supported by the width of you, eating raspberries squashed between layers of waffle: messy and delicious like your mouth, and our bed where later – between your legs – we'd locked into each other's bodies with the pink stain of raspberry juice still on our fingers.

8

One Wednesday Ellie and Mira persuade me to perform at the open mic at The White Rabbit, the one we'd stumbled into after the first book club. I'm nervous but the girls just laugh at me.

'Babe, literally nothing could go wrong.'

'Chill out and eat your chicken.'

By the time I perform they've both had so much gin they'll think anything I do is great. I'm glad; I need it not to matter how this goes; I've just got to do it. I close my eyes and sing and as soon as I've started I don't feel out of practice anymore. When I get to the chorus and open my eyes I half expect you to be there dancing in front of me, smiling, all twisting limbs and hard, heady love. I see the girls instead, giving me a thumbs-up and waving from the corner.

9

The book club come over for dinner on the night before my birthday. We order a massive Indian takeaway, and Noel brings Jim, Jackie brings her husband and Duane, Sean and Talin all come too.

We squeeze into our living room and drink wine out of mugs. We eat Peshwari naan and lamb bhuna and vegetable biriani with samosas and saag aloo. I tuck in between Danny's knees and Jackie whips out a cake with candles that we light with Ellie's lighter, and they all sing 'Happy Birthday'.

After we've eaten we persuade Frank to do some magic and he tells us a story using props he plucks out of mid-air. I ask him to do the fire trick he'd started by accident in Germany and he says we'll have to save it for another time. Then the hat in his hand starts smoking and he waves it around to beat up the flames and put them out again.

When he's finished everyone drifts home, and we have to ban Jackie from doing any of the washing up in order to send her away. I stay in the sitting room with Ellie and Mira and the boys until midnight: smoking and finishing off the wine. At midnight the others say happy birthday and go off to bed, and Danny and I stay curled up together on the sofa. He kisses me and I put my feet onto his, feeling the rough wool of his socks warming up my bare toes.

He says, 'What's in your brain, Holly?' and pushes his fingers into the skin of my forehead.

I don't know whether it's OK to tell him so instead I brush his fingers away with my head. I move it closer to him so my face is touching his.

'When you were little, what did you want to be when you grew up?' I ask.

'A farmer.'

'Are you being serious?'

'Yeah. I always wanted to own my own cow.'

'But you're such a town boy.'

'What are you talking about? I'm from the seaside. Really, I should've been a surfer.'

I laugh at him and he slides his hand around my back and pulls the rest of me in close.

'You feeling old, birthday girl?' he asks.

'I don't know what I'm feeling. Tired.'

We lie there for a bit with his hand resting in the small of my back.

'You know I could've been a farmer,' I say. 'I sheared a sheep once.'

'What?'

'Yeah. One of my friends lived on a farm and his dad let me help with the shearing once.'

'Ah that's right, I always forget you're actually a Surrey girl. You're not really a Londoner at all, you're a country bumpkin.'

'Shut your face,' I say, and he kisses me.

'Go on, tell me about shearing the sheep.'

'Well I thought it'd be fun but the sheep really didn't like it. You have to kind of sit on them to keep them still and they get really distressed.'

'Foolish sheep. How could anyone mind you sitting on them?'

I laugh and kiss him, wrapping myself up in his legs and the sofa.

Later we go upstairs to bed, and I stand in the bathroom cleaning my teeth, thinking about you standing next to me cleaning yours. After Danny has gone to sleep I lie awake for a while, thinking about the birthday card in the bottom drawer of my desk and your stiff handwriting etched inside it. I know exactly what it says and imagine you whispering it in my ear as I lie there.

I haven't been sleeping naked, so in the morning Danny slides a hand under my top and rolls my left nipple through his finger and thumb. I've missed waking up with you behind me. Danny likes to touch my nipples a lot more than you did; you used your tongue on them but I like this too. I turn around to face him and find the line of his buttocks through his boxer shorts with my fingers. He asks me if I'm OK and I nod, and he slides down the bed to kiss my hips and the edge of my knickers. I put my fingers in his hair but when he takes off my underwear I start doing times tables in my head.

When I pull him up and kiss him, I can taste my saltiness on his lips. His eyes are closed and he's frowning slightly. The joke about the duck who walks into the bar and keeps asking for bread is in my head and I start laughing. He opens his eyes and looks at me like he's a bit concerned so I say, 'Sorry, I was thinking about that joke with the duck and the bread.'

He goes to say something but I climb on top of him and push my mouth quite hard against his. I feel as though our gums are squishing together. I'm still sort of laughing into his mouth and I'm kissing him hard at the same time. I know I need to get it together but I also really want to push my finger into his belly button and then smell it, or bite his nose really hard, or do something that means I get to touch him but that isn't this.

Instead I push my mouth into his shoulder and move my hips so that the top of his penis is in the right place for sex. I push down on him and he puts his hands on my back and pulls my body in to slow it down. He asks me again if I'm OK and he's smiling, but it's obviously confusing for him that I'm still sort of laughing about the joke. I am OK though and I feel calmer now. I say sorry but he shakes his head and kisses me. Everything stops for a minute. It's like lots of flying ants take off from under the skin on my shoulders and leave me breathing better. It's already familiar with him – his body and his mouth – and I don't have to pretend this time; I come just before he does.

I understand how ivy feels, wanting to stay tangled up in him for the rest of the day like green creeping limbs around a tree trunk. We doze.

When I wake up again I find my towel and kiss him before I go to the bathroom. I stand in the shower, crying quietly and not understanding how I feel.

10

My family come down to take me out for lunch. I don't invite Danny and we don't talk about it; he just goes home. I hope he doesn't feel sad. I'm trying to be careful with him, with myself, while this in-between space hovers. But I don't know what I'm doing.

I walk along the front with Mum and Dad and Rob and we

eat pizza at Alfresco, watching the sky dance with the sea. I laugh at Rob's impressions of Lucy planning the wedding and not everything upsets me. I feel guilty about that. Your mum phones me in the afternoon after they've left and I sit on the beach talking to her. Her voice is still thick with pain and I'm confused. Of course I wish you were here, Sam, but you can't be. I've forgiven you for that. Don't be angry with me.

It's the middle of the Brighton Fringe so walking home the roads are packed with people flyering and playing music, and I take a few leaflets from people wearing face paint and walking round on stilts. Some of the kids I teach at school are in a show with a community theatre group. I should find out where it is and go see it.

I sit in my room that night listening to the bikutsi music that reminds me of you. I keep putting off starting *Jude* because I'm not sure if it will still be painful. I hope it would. I don't want to stop missing you.

11

I go running that night, down the middle of the roads where there aren't any shadows. There's a stillness in the dark that gets inside me like music, and the air is easier to breathe. It makes me tired though. I like it better when running makes me feel strong: the power in my body, the speed I've built up and the familiarity of the pavements. The corners carry me round them and push me onwards.

Running in the daytime lets the world feel transient. I move along unfazed by the conversations walking past because I'm gone before I get caught up in them. Sometimes this is something I need. I'm scared to feel settled in case I get stuck. There are things I don't want to lose and I get tired when I think about it.

Tonight I listen to the silence and the wind and worry about everything being gone. My feet hit the ground hard and it hurts. When I get home Ellie is sitting up in the kitchen with a cup of coffee.

'You're not meant to be out all night, Holly. It's unnatural, unless you're on drugs or having crazy al fresco sex.'

I smile at her.

'I couldn't sleep.'

'Yeah me neither. Want to come stay in my room?'

I nod and we go upstairs and in the morning she wakes me up with a cup of tea.

'How are your muscles?' she says.

'A bit achy.'

'A bit sad?'

'Yeah.'

'It's because you're old now; that's what birthdays do.'

We curl up together, sipping our tea. We don't say anything; we let the morning be what it is.

12

It's 3rd June and it's been a year since you died. I phone your mum and your sister and then spend the rest of the day at the viaduct with Frank. We make sure to shout a thank you to Edward the architect again as we leave to go home, and Frank drives us back too quickly down the wide roads. I swim that night, and the sea is cold and wild. My parents call before bed.

'It's just another day,' I tell them. 'There's nothing to say.'

13

I've been invited to sports day at the school where I run my choir. I'm always there on Tuesdays anyway and all the kids who sing with me will be racing. They ask me if I'm going to come, 'Go on, Miss, it'll be really fun. You can be on our team if you want.'

When I say I will, the head asks if the choir can perform, and we get a bunch of songs ready for the parents. Danny books the afternoon off work to come too. He's being supportive and it's sweet but there's something in me that feels claustrophobic; I don't know if I'm ready for us to live in each other's daytimes. I know I'm not being fair; we wake up together most mornings and find each other at night. The longer it goes on the more confused I feel.

He looks at me like I'm somewhere he wants to settle and I want him to be a place I escape to. I think he must be a runaway too, or I don't know why Frank would have found him. But he holds me like my skin was made to feel his fingers and his breath and I'm scared I can't do that anymore. He asks me to love him with his eyes and I feel like all I am is empty space.

14

I still clean the cream house on Tuesdays. It still makes me angry with its locked drawers and mirrors.

Today I listen to a podcast about comets while I work and imagine the walls are the curves of a spaceship. I don't follow all of it and I like a lot of the ideas that are wrong more than the ones the scientists say are maybe right. They talk about something called panspermia. I like the word, and write it down on a little piece of paper. I put it in my purse next to the fact you told me once about four-sided shapes: whatever kind of quadrangle you draw, if you connect up their midpoints you'll always get a perfect parallelogram.

One of the people on the podcast says that comets are like frozen time capsules, with stuff in them from when the solar system had just formed. I like that thought, that if we could crack one open we'd find a message from the start of time.

When I was at school we buried a time capsule in our school field to mark the new millennium. Every class had to choose something to put in it and the headmaster wrote a letter that went in too, wrapped in a plastic bag. He read it to us in assembly, and we all had to write our own 'Letter to the Future' in English class. Mr Jenkins's was the only one that went in the time capsule though. I remember listening to it and thinking that if I'd found it in a thousand years I'd have been pretty disappointed. It didn't have any jokes in it and it just said a lot of stuff about our school values. I felt quite doubtful about the whole thing; when I'd accidentally left bits of my sandwich in a plastic bag they went mouldy in just a few days so I didn't really think that a letter – which I was sure was less resilient than a sandwich – was going to last for hundreds of years. But when we recorded our school song to put in there too, I sung really loudly just in case.

I wish you'd left a time capsule for me, something I could hold now I can't hold onto you. I'll hold Danny's hand later. Your hands were bigger than mine, thicker. His are bony and wide.

I feel a bit panicky as I lock up the house and walk into school, but I take comfort in the fact that even the wonkiest quadrangle makes a parallelogram. Sometimes I guess you just have to keep on going to find out what the future's meant to be.

15

The sun is out. At school, Danny's waiting for me. I smile into his face and he reminds me of things that end: a different man who spills out of me when I laugh. I look into his eyes and see you splattered in front of me. He makes a joke about the parents waiting nervously on the sidelines and it's funny. I pull him in and kiss him.

'Thank you for coming,' I say, and I mean it.

The races at school go on all afternoon and the kids sing at the end before a big sit-down barbecue with the parents and staff. We're outside for all of it, in a big field behind the playground. The sky is so high up and so blue. It's impossible not to enjoy it with summer bursting in on us.

One of the boys in my choir wins the whole-school 100 metres and he sits opposite me and Danny to eat.

'I'm pretty fast, aren't I, Miss? I'm probably going to be in the Olympics when I grow up.'

'You are fast, Luke, yeah. Do you want to be in the 100 metres?'

'No, I want to do gymnastics. I'm even better at backflips than I am at running. I'm really good.'

He gets up and runs off to find his dad. Danny laughs and I squeeze his hand under the table. He looks at me with mischief in his eyes.

'What?' he says.

'You can't laugh at him; he's so earnest. Don't crush his dreams.'

Danny laughs at me then and kisses me and doesn't care that people can see.

'You're so sweet with them,' he says.

Afterwards, as we're getting our stuff together to go home, the girl who'd been sitting next to Luke comes over to me. I don't know her name – she isn't in the choir – but she'd looked upset and worried all through my conversation with Luke so I ask her if there's anything wrong.

She says, 'I'm not fast enough for the Olympics, Miss.'

She looks on the verge of tears.

'Don't worry about that, poppet; not many people are,' I reply. 'I'm sure there are other things you're good at.'

'I don't think there are, Miss. I don't know what I want to be when I grow up and everybody else does.'

'Well it's a difficult decision to make. What things do you like to do?'

'I like looking after my little sister and I like aeroplanes, but I don't know if I'd be very good at driving one.'

'That's OK. The thing is you don't have to decide right now. To be honest you'll probably end up trying lots of different things. I still don't really know what I want to do yet.'

She looks confused. 'But you're a teacher aren't you, Miss? You teach the singing club.'

On the way back to the car Danny holds my hand. Our palms sweat into each other. He says, 'You do know what you want to do, Holly. You're a musician. When are you going to start doing that?'

I look at him and I can see myself how he sees me. I'm a singer, and I'm beautiful, and I'm someone capable of all this love. It's what I've been looking for: somewhere calm to stop. There's this stillness all around us, but I'm even more lost than I was before. I don't see the woman who's in his eyes when I look in the mirror; I see a girl who's ashamed and confused and trying to find out who she can be when she's alone.

We drive back to Danny's. That night in his bed, he uses his mouth on me and I feel my spine stiffen. I try to make myself smaller. I wrap around him like I'm a swimming pool he's moving through. When he touches me he can't tell this is a part of me that hurts. You are curled up inside me. When we move like this I feel so lonely. He uses his tongue to find the wet between my legs and holds my hand while I think about you.

I don't want him to catch my sadness, so I roll over after he's been inside me, with my face to the wall.

16

Frank texts me in the week to say he has a surprise for me. He says to come to his house that evening if I can.

It's been a beautiful day and now the sunset's filling the sky the colour of orange juice and grenadine. I walk along the prom from Hove where I've been cleaning. There are people filling the beach like crabs and someone with a guitar and a smooth candlelight voice is busking at the bar by the sailing club. I cut up to Frank's when I get to the pier and wind through the streets to his house.

Frank opens the door and starts to lead me into his kitchen.

'Before you panic, I just had it tuned for you. I got it for free from someone who wanted to throw it away. But I got fed up with hearing you talk about playing and I wanted to hear for myself so . . .'

He opens the door and along the wall opposite the oven and the sink there's a piano. I look at him in disbelief and he laughs.

'Play me something?'

He puts the kettle on and I pull a chair up to the piano and open the lid. It has a beautiful sound and by the time Frank's made the tea I can just about speak enough to say thank you.

I play Frank all the things I can't say. I play my confusion and my sadness. I play feeling better and feeling lost and wanting so much to keep running. I play the guilt that sticks to my lips like red-wine stains and the hangover of you I'm stuck breathing in. I play the wind and the sea and wanting to fly away.

17

Most evenings I stay at Danny's or he stays at mine. I start to feel cramped. I spent so long wanting to wrap around a body and now I go days without sleeping. I don't think he knows this. He lies next to me and I peel the day from out under my fingernails. I pull at the skin around the edges of my fingers until they bleed. I play a game where I try not to let their bleeding get on the bed sheets. When it does I feel bad.

In the morning he always makes me a cup of tea; there are too many holes in my bones for me to hold liquid but I drink it. I wash him off in the shower and write songs about you when he leaves. He doesn't know this, that I am a cave: a hollowed-out rock full of the dark. I love you. I don't know what to do with this missing.

On Saturdays Mira makes scrambled eggs, and we all sit and eat together with croissants and tomatoes. I'll put my new lyrics to music and try not to think about my skin and the way it wants to rub against someone else's. The way I want to peel it off altogether. Then Danny makes me laugh, or draws a picture on my spine, or I see something I need to tell him and I feel full again and safe.

He smiles at me from across the room when we all go to the pub together; he replies to every message I send him. I worry about him when he's tired from work or anxious about a deadline and I like the way his mouth nuzzles into mine.

I go to Frank's almost every morning before work and play it all out on the piano. Some days he has requests for songs he wants to hear and he sits next to me and sings along. Other days he's acquired some sheet music somewhere and asks me to try it out. After a while I offer to teach him, and I start giving him lessons twice a week. Magic has left his hands nimble and strong and he quickly picks up the basic techniques. He struggles with reading music but he has a good ear so we mostly abandon that and I teach him pieces by memory.

Sometimes Frank talks about Ian; sometimes he pushes his

hands through the wood of the piano like it's air and pulls out a picture of Ian laughing, or walking through the woods, or curled in bed. I won't know where it's come from. He'll say, 'Let's play a song about this today,' and I'll laugh because I still don't understand how he makes things appear from nothing.

We both need the music, relishing the stories it holds in the quiet morning lull. We need each other too.

18

It's our party at the end of June and my friends are mostly heading down to Brighton from London after work; they start to trickle in around 9-ish. We're all a bit pissed and high already so everything feels kind of sepia-toned and easy, and Mira's made the kind of playlist that everyone wants to stay in the kitchen dancing to all night. Ellie and Sean have always lived in Brighton so lots of their friends get there early and soon our house is packed.

The evening is a montage of greatest hits and snapshot conversations. At one point I'm sat outside in our back yard with my friends from home, smoking and talking about nothing.

'Fuck, Hols, it's been way too long.'

'This place is sick; now you've had us down here this summer will basically just be us crashing every weekend.'

'Oh God, it's so good to get out of London.'

'It's so good to see you.'

'We've missed you.'

'We've missed Sam.'

'Are you OK?'

We all sit there and cry together and smoke a joint and talk about how beautiful you were. Then we go in and dance and drink and rub our bodies together and hold hands and fall in love with the world and cry and dance and swirl around in it all, feeling broken and gorgeous and alive, and wishing you were too.

Back in the kitchen – later sometime – Mira comes over and puts her arms round me.

'Holly, did you know that Danny's gone home?'

'What? No, I didn't. Why did he go?'

'I'm not sure; I thought maybe you two'd had a fight.'

'No, I've barely seen him.'

She nods and flicks my nose as though to say *don't worry*, and something comes on through the speakers that makes her throw up her arms. She grabs my hands and pulls me into the crowd of dancing and I forget about everything else.

I wake up the next morning on our living-room floor, wrapped up in a duvet that I must have gone and got from my room. There are empty bottles and glasses with dregs of liquid in them strewn across the floor. There are a bunch of cigarette ends in the glass of water that I'd obviously got for myself at some point the night before. I notice they're straights and wonder if we popped out to get some or if they're someone else's. I go upstairs to find Ellie and she and Sean are sitting up in her bed awake and talking but looking a bit fragile.

'Good morning, my little beauty,' Ellie says.

'Oh my God, I feel so far from beautiful it's unreal.'

We laugh and they make room for me on the bed.

'Sean, do you know why Danny left last night?'

They look at each other.

'You've got to talk to him about it, Holly,' he says.

'I know; I'm sorry. I just don't remember that much of the evening and I don't know where my phone is and I'm worried I did something horrible.'

'You weren't horrible at all, you were hilarious. But I think Danny just wasn't sure where he fitted into it all and that's a conversation you need to have with him and not us.'

Ellie puts her arms round me.

'Did you sleep downstairs? How's the rest of the house?'

'It's a bit of a state but it'll be fine. We just need to get everyone on it for a couple of hours.'

'Sean brought a disposable barbecue over last night and we thought we could chuck everyone out for some bacon and sausages on the beach after the clean-up.'

'The dream.'

I snuggle in with them for a bit and my head hurts and I hope that Danny got home OK.

19

The worst thing about a hangover for me is anxiety. I wake up the morning after I've been drinking – especially if the night before's a bit patchy – and I feel tense. It's like the top of my head has come off and my thoughts are sitting just above it, so I can't quite make them make sense, and the rest of my body feels frantic because I'm not in it.

Normally you found my worrying annoying but – after nights out – if you'd woken up before me you'd see I was stirring and you'd get me a cup of tea with sugar in it. Before I asked you you'd tell me I hadn't done anything to panic about. You'd let me lie tucked up in your body and you'd put your chin on my head because you knew it made me feel like you were pushing me back inside my skin again, and you'd kiss me and you'd tell me you loved me, and you wouldn't mind that I needed to hear it. We'd eat breakfast in bed at lunchtime and we'd stay there all day feeling safe and being silly and sweating out the poison watching crap TV.

20

After a late breakfast on the beach our friends walked back off up the hill to the train station or went home, and I walked into town to bum around for a bit with Duane and Mira. Sean and Ellie went back to bed and the house was mostly clean but I still hadn't found my phone so I hadn't spoken to Danny. I text him on Mira's phone and hoped he'd get in touch; Mum and Dad and Rob and Lucy were coming down for dinner and Danny was potentially coming too, but I felt too grimy and hungover to really think about it.

'Shall we just go to the pub?' Duane says. I wince and Mira laughs.

'Hair of the dog I guess.'

It was a day that looked cold but not so much you needed a coat. I felt my skin getting revived by the outside as we walked along the street. The bacon had made me feel a bit better, like if I was sick now at least I would have something to throw up. The excess of people around me seemed messier than I felt, so the chaos was making me feel calmer. We sat outside the Komedia and drank pints and laughed about what we remembered from the night before.

After about an hour Danny phones and asks me to meet him by the seafront so I split from the others and walk down to find him.

I get there after him and as I approach the bench I think about how strange it is that a year ago I didn't know any of them. It's the same bench where Frank stopped to tell me I'd dropped my keys and I look down instinctively to see if there's anything on the floor. There's a flower there, a single blue stem, and I pick it up and don't know what to think.

Danny stands up and kisses me on the cheek. We sit down next to each other.

'I'm sorry I left last night.'

'That's OK. We missed you though. Were you alright?'

'I just didn't know what I was doing there. None of your friends knew who I was and I didn't know if I was meant to tell them I was your boyfriend. We were all pissed and it wasn't the right time to talk about it so I went home. I just need to know how you feel.'

I look at Danny and then I look at the beach. There's a group of kids playing with a dog. Out at sea a couple of windsurfers are scooting along the top of the water. I think about how windsurfing would be a good thing to try and learn while I'm living here.

'Ellie always says that adults are just bigger, uglier versions of children,' I say. 'That stuff is hard at our age because we still think that one day soon we'll be a grown-up and know what to do about things so we spend the whole time feeling frustrated and confused we're not there yet. She reckons it never actually happens but we all just get better at feeling OK about that.'

'It's a good theory.'

The dog runs into the sea and out again and shakes itself off on the beach, covering the children in spray. One of the boys starts crying and a woman sitting further up the beach tries to decide whether she needs to go and comfort him. One of the windsurfers falls off and I draw my coat in around me as the wind brushes over.

'Are you cold?'

'No, I'm OK.' I look at him. 'Danny, I really like you but I can't be your girlfriend. I'm sorry.'

He grips his thighs and then pushes his hands down his legs and onto his knees.

'I'm really sorry, I wanted it to work. I thought that it would. I'm just not there yet.'

He nods and stands up. He looks like he's trying to decide whether to say something else. It reminds me of the night we walked home together after playing football at the viaduct, and I think about all the places where I'd still like to kiss him.

'I know it's still hard for you sometimes, Holly, but I thought this meant something more to you. I don't know what to say; I think you've been a bit of a dick.'

'I'm sorry.'

He nods again. I stand up too and hug him and he pats me on the back. I step back and he turns and walks away. I feel sad but I know it's the right thing because when I turn around and stand there looking out at the sea, I'm thinking about you.

I go back to Frank's and wait there for my family to arrive for dinner. I tell him what happened but I feel like he already knows and then I play the piano to him and the music washes away some of the stuff I don't want to be there. We sip tea and eat cake and I wonder why it was that Frank found Danny, what magic it was that he needed.

21

In the evenings after dinner Ellie and Mira and I sit up chatting. I think about you more than ever. I don't feel sad, mostly, but I've started to want to talk about you more.

'It's nice to get to know Sam after all this time, Holly Jones,' Ellie says. 'He sounds like a treat.'

One night, I just come out with it, the thought that's been too painful to say, that's sat in the space beneath my ribcage since the coroner decided your death was a tragic accident.

'One thing that gets at me,' I say, 'is I don't get how it happened. He was always so careful and I don't understand why he didn't look before crossed. Sometimes I wonder whether –'

I can't finish the sentence and I'm really crying, like I'm stood by the side of the road again with my dad and the cars streaming past and the pain stopping me from moving anywhere because I'm thinking about how hard it would be to get hit accidentally, how you could possibly just walk out into the road in a York suburb and not realise a car with a woman called Elizabeth Whitworth in it was coming at you at 40 mph, and why, if you had realised, you didn't try to stop.

'You can't think like that, poppet,' Ellie says. 'That's your grief giving you shit to keep you up at night. I just don't believe that thought is true.'

I feel like a child.

'But what if it is?'

'Even if Sam woke up one morning and the world felt like too much for him, the only thing you'll ever know for sure is what you had was beautiful.'

Mira slides along the sofa and puts her arm round me, 'You've got to hold onto that bit, Holly.'

22

I think one of the worst feelings in the world – and by this I don't mean emotions, I mean tactile things, and some good ones for me are rolling in sand, although not everyone likes this, or silk underwear, or sun on something which doesn't often feel it, the belly maybe, things you touch, things you feel physically and that reach your brain as a feather or a cloud of settling icing sugar or a cold metal spoon on the tongue – one of the worst feelings in the world is water on the thighs from the inner rim of a public toilet: the splash from the flush, which has settled on the seat and attached itself to the bend in your leg that moves from your vagina round to your buttocks.

You haven't noticed it as you've stood up and now it's trapped in by a pair of tights and turned into a dampness on your upper back thighs that clings there, the reminder of someone else's urine and a strange wetness with nothing to do with exertion – sexual or otherwise – and clumps lankly, stationary, like molecules of fat, or little pieces of mould inside a sandwich box you forgot to put in the dishwasher.

It's not pleasant in the slightest, it's the opposite; it's disgusting and repulsive and it's horrible; it gives me goose bumps and makes me need to wash, or at the very least wipe, but it isn't the kind of wetness you can wipe off or even dry because, like I said, once it's there, it's damp and dank. It lurks, and it's frightening.

It has been over a year, Sam, and I have only just stopped feeling like there is someone else's regurgitated toilet water wrapped around my heart and filling up the gaps.

And I love you, Sam – so much – but I hope you know how absolutely horrible that's made me feel.

23

Gabriella and I have been experimenting all summer with making ice cream and we've succeeded with a phenomenal pistachio and a slightly less good strawberry. The weekend after Wimbledon I've gone over to help her cook for a party she's helping Talin hold for Cora's fifth birthday. We decide to have another go at the strawberry in a bid to make Neopolitan and I arrive with several cartons of milk and a bag of fresh fruit. I can tell when I arrive Gabriella's upset; she's slicing things unevenly and fast, and she's distracted when I speak to her. I wonder if maybe she's had a fight with Talin. When I ask her what's wrong she answers in a tired voice.

'Zimmerman was found not guilty of murder yesterday, Holly. I'm feeling a bit angry.'

I hadn't really known about the story but I'd watched the reactions unfold on twitter the day before so I know what she means.

'In the Trayvon Matthews case, right?'

She looks at me, 'Trayvon Martin.'

'Right, of course. Sorry.'

'That's OK, Holly; it's not your problem, is it? What does it matter to you what his name is?'

She puts the radio on. It's a bit tense, but after a while something comes on that we both like and we sing along a bit. The recipe is pretty simple – it's just the timings we messed up before – so soon we're done, and we sit outside in her garden with glasses of water from the fridge.

'I'm sorry about before, Gabriella,' I say. 'I'm an idiot.'

'You don't get a free pass because your boyfriend was black,' she says, with a wry smile.

'I know,' I reply. 'I am sorry about what happened. He was really young, wasn't he?'

'Seventeen. Same as Joseph would have been.'

She tops up my water from a jug and looks at me. She's sad and when she speaks it's heavy, like it costs a lot to be saying it.

'I just think attention should be paid, you know.'

24

On 17th July I'm offered a job as the education assistant at the Theatre Royal Brighton. I tell my piano students I'll teach them until the summer holidays, and one of the music teachers says she'll keep my choir going at school. I'm really sad to leave them all. I even feel a bit nostalgic as I clean the cream house for the last time and dust down the locked drawers I've never seen inside of. It feels like a real start though, putting down some roots.

I'm with Gabriella when I get the job offer, and we go out for wine. I drink one glass and feel a bit tipsy so I don't order another one. I walk home slowly thinking about new things.

Later, I wander down to the St James that night to meet the others for the quiz and I look out over the sea from Kemptown. There are things I really love here. I know one day they might all disappear but I don't feel scared. I feel happy, and I know there'll be sadness in tomorrow and happiness in tomorrow but underneath the emotions, which will always keep changing, I feel safe.

25

We have a heatwave, and Brighton sags with the weight of day trippers swelling on the beach.

During the week I love the bustle that the heat brings. The terraces of the clubs along the front fill with evening drinkers in flip-flops and T-shirts chucked on over bikinis. We all meet after work just west of the bandstand and lie on the stones in the end of the light. Danny and I bring our guitars down, and we sing a bit or sit around and talk about nothing.

It's soon the school summer holidays and my new job means co-ordinating the community workshops set up for local children as a summer club. A couple of my kids from school are down at the theatre learning circus skills and I go and see them at lunchtime to hear what they're up to.

'It's great, Miss, we're learning how to walk on the tight-rope.'

'Hold onto that,' I say. 'It's a useful skill.'

I'm gigging too, singing at little acoustic nights and writing songs most weekends. One day Sean and Ellie come down and watch my set and afterwards Sean says I should come into the studio with him in September and lay down some tracks for an EP. Ellie takes me for champagne at the Mercure to celebrate.

Danny and I don't often get together just us anymore but he's started seeing a girl from work. I sometimes feel sad that his stillness and mine didn't quite sit together right, but things are OK between us.

At the weekends – when the town is fat with tourists sweating on every street corner – I lie in a deckchair on Frank's roof and fall asleep in the heat reading a book, or go for a run in the dry air, the sun beating my skin into action. When my drink runs out of ice Frank shakes it and it fills back up.

Some days we sit with the day's papers and the world feels like it's getting too hot. Frank paces round the roof looking at the sky and the headlines, and frowns. I dissect them with Gabriella over summer trifles and sweet, crispy salads. She tells me I've become an expert at fresh pea soup.

I know that you would have loved this heat. In the mornings when I get up early for work I can almost feel you moving around in the kitchen with me as I boil my egg or pour my cereal. I miss you most when the sun is setting. I can see your body lazing in our back yard on Sunday afternoons with Duane and Sean as they tune into the cricket. I sometimes feel sad there aren't any people here who remember you too, and I still want to talk about you more as the memories become less bitter. I decide that when I've settled into my job I'll go back up to York and see your family again. I invite Alfie and Danielle to stay with me too, and they say they'll come at the end of August.

26

I meet up with Rob and Lucy in London for lunch one Saturday, and afterwards we leave Rob to go elsewhere while I look at wedding dresses with Lucy and her other bridesmaids. At one point – while Lucy's in the changing room – one of them asks me if I will be bringing a partner to the wedding and at first I go to give my default answer that my boyfriend was hit by a car and died.

I stop myself before it comes out though. I look at her instead and say, 'No, it'll just be me.'

After we've been shopping I stay over at Rob and Lucy's place. We watch old episodes of *West Wing* and they tell me about their plans to go to Australia on their honeymoon. As we go to bed Rob hugs me.

'You're quite a woman you know, Holly. You grew up good.'

I laugh at him, but I fall asleep wondering if I was a woman before; when it was that I grew up? I think about how one day I'll be seventy-seven like Frank and you'll still be twenty-seven and I'm sad we won't get full and wrinkly together; I'm sad we don't get to see each other grow. I hope I was a woman when you knew me too; you were a wonderful man.

27

We all chipped in for a cheap barbecue at the start of July and at least once a week through August we drag it down to the beach and cook burgers and sausages, or kebabs and fish if we're feeling more adventurous. Sometimes people we don't know come over and join us, bringing food or bottles of beer and we all sit round in what feels like a hot pause, where nothing is real and the air is hazy and secretive and full of perspiration. The seawater is cold and blue and I float in it on my back, letting the sun catch its flecks in the hair on my skin like tiny pieces of mirror. I like feeling salty as I get out, lying on the beach in my underwear and eating dripping slabs of halloumi out of a paper napkin.

Frank says that as summer winds down through August it always feels like a new year to him. He used to travel so much when he was working that I think he finds it hard sometimes, living in one place and just watching the rhythms of the seasons. I think I know what he means, and I wonder if I'll feel like him when it's autumn again and the chlorophyll is draining from the leaves, urging him to move on and find a new audience for his magic. But we have the sea and – like he told me on the day he first found me – when you sit by the water it really does feel like things will be alright.

28

I find the melody for the song about our night in Rome when the heat breaks and the thunder sets in. It's a Monday evening and I'm walking home from work. The sea swirls and groans and I think about what it would feel like to swim in it.

It's pouring with rain, but I go to the beach and I lie down and look at the water falling out of the sky at me. I stand up and strip down to my underwear and hobble to the edge of the water. The stones under my feet mean I walk in jerks, my body twisting and settling with each step. I test the water with my ankles and I plunge in. The waves knock me over again and again and I climb back into them and let them toss me up and grind me back down into the stones. I am laughing and dancing and I feel like the sea is in me, even though I'm in it, and I scramble out, bruised and with cuts on my elbows and knees. I use my jumper to dry off a bit and I pull my jeans and my T-shirt back on and it's sad and it's beautiful.

I run to Frank's because I know I have the song in my head now and I want to try it out on the piano, but he makes me have a warm shower and a cup of tea before he'll let me play. I sing him the song and my fingers spread out over the new melody and he sits with tears in his eyes. When I finish he says, 'I knew that you were a magician when I met you.'

And I say, 'No, Frank, the magic is all yours.'

29

In September Ellie, Mira and I are going to stop smoking. We've decided we need a holiday so we're going to put the money we'd have spent on tobacco and Rizlas in a jar in the kitchen and save up for Eurostar tickets to Paris. We're going to walk along by the Seine and drink coffee in cafes on crisp winter evenings and speak French. I'm going to read *Jude the Obscure* while we're there and I'll probably hate it.

I've been thinking about starting a band and I have the EP to think about next month too. When I mentioned it to Frank he said that when I start making music videos I should remember how good he is at dancing.

Danielle and Alfie are arriving next week and I'm going to take them into the arcades on the pier and take Alfie on the ghost train. I've told your mum I'll come and visit her soon too, but she's off on a cruise in September and Danielle says she's been getting involved with their local Sunday school. I think she's OK too, Sam. I hope you are.

I sometimes get the train into London and walk around and smell the air. I can see your face on the breath of the city and I can feel you like sweat on my palms: memories of your skin print on a street corner. And London is the same as it always is and I trace your patterns in it.

But I can't smell you anymore, Sam. Everything just smells of the city and you're gone so all I can find on my pillow and my toothbrush when I go home to Brighton again is me. I sometimes sit and cut things up: bits of paper into other bits of paper I don't really know what to do with. I stand and watch the sea and think about going travelling or how I don't really know what I want to do with my life. I remember what Frank said about the fact I can't put it in a box or paint it purple and I go round to Gabriella's house instead and make goat's cheese and beetroot balls. Most days I'm fine.

But, Sam, I can feel you in the air by the sea when I stand

and let the waves get inside me. I look at them crashing down on the beach, breathing and tumbling with something like a voice inside them, and even though the wonky tooth in the bottom row of your smile is just ash in the wind now, and I can't remember what you smell like, I find you there in the water, and we fly up into the air like kites.

Acknowledgements

Thank you to Aki Shilz for permission to use her poem for the epigraph. Aki's poetry and her brilliant work with Losslit is on Twitter @AkiShilz. Thank you also to Denise Riley for kind permission to reprint the lines from her poem 'Shantung' on page 63. 'Shantung' was originally published in *Mop Mop Georgette* (Reality Street, 1993).

To Laura West, you have made me a better writer and made this a much better book. I am enormously grateful for everything you've done and continue to do for me; thank you so much. Thank you Nikki Griffiths for believing in me and for giving this book its chance at real life. Thanks too to the extended teams at David Higham Associates and Melville House, including Marina Drukman for her beautiful cover design.

Thank you for the creative and professional development offered me by the teams at Mslexia Novel Competition and the Northern Writers Award; Spread the Word, in particular Laura Kenwright; Roundhouse London, especially Sylvia Harrison and Bohdan Piasesci; Cityread; the Soho Society, particularly Clare Lynch; and #Losslit. Thank you to my teachers Gaye Penfold, who encouraged me to write; Dr Kathryn Murphy, who taught me so much about reading; and Sarah Branston, who nurtured my imagination and resilience. From my time at Goldsmiths, thank you to Vicky Macleroy, Ardu Vashil and my MA group's feedback and encouragement. Thanks in particular to Belinda Zhawi, my partner in crime from that time. To all my friends, colleagues and mentors who've supported me through this process, thank you so much. I'd like to acknowledge Jasmine Cooray, Toni Stuart, Miriam Nash, Dr Maria Neophytou, Dr Nathalie Teitler, Arabella Lawson, Phoebe Sparrow, Guy Macines-Manby, Ali Livesey, Dean Atta, Linda Biney, Kate Phillips, Sahar Halaimzai, Antosh Wojcik, Sophie Fenella, Matt Simmonds and Sarah Coveney.

Thank you especially to early readers Sarah Anson and Sarah Chesshyre, who read through the night way back at the beginning, and to Ben Perry who told me what needed to happen to make it work. Thank you to Dr Georgie Torlot for talking me the through the medical bits, and to Jake Perry for checking my French.

Thank you to my extended family for your continued support: the Torlots, Jacksons, Plummers, Stallards, Reads, Marshalls, et al. To Genevieve Dawson, Lewis Turner, Rachel Diamond-Hunter and Michael Diamond-Hunter, thank you for being my team; I'm so grateful. Kayo Chingonyi, you've been so generous and patient throughout this process; for being my partner and my friend, thank you so much. To the Perrys: Dad, Mum, Jake and Ben, thank you for your unwavering support, encouragement and love. This would never have happened without you.

Reading Group Guide

1. Some believe the process of grief has five stages: denial, anger, bargaining, depression, and acceptance. How does Holly's experience with the loss of Sam fit into these stages?

2. Early on in the book Holly describes Frank's book group as 'a collection of broken people.' Is this all that brings them together, and whose untold story are you most interested in?

3. Sometimes Holly's overwhelming feelings of grief mean she behaves in selfish ways. Did that make her seem more human to you, or harder to like? Is it necessary to like a novel's protagonist?

4. Holly is about to turn twenty-three when Sam dies. How is her experience of grief altered by her young age?

5. When Rob gives Holly a watch, he says that he 'doesn't believe time makes stuff better, we have to make it better for ourselves.' What are Holly's ways of trying to make things better, and in what ways does she struggle?

6. How did you feel about the way Holly ended things with Danny? Was it a good idea for him to try and

have a relationship with her, knowing what she was experiencing?

7. The novel is a record of all the things Holly imagines saying to Sam as she processes his absence. How does it feel to access these private thoughts, and what do you think of Sam as a character?

8. There is a lot of cooking and eating in the novel. How do food and grief interact for Holly?

9. Holly chooses to have casual sex twice in the novel, both times when she's been drinking. What do you think her motivation is, and how is it related to her broader experience of her sexuality now Sam has died?

10. The Monty Hall problem is presented as a way for Holly to explain how she gets angry at things she cannot understand, yet later on Frank says that magic is one of the few things that makes people happier when they don't understand it. What does Frank's magic add to the novel and did you believe in it?

Author Bio

S.K. PERRY was shortlisted in the Mslexia Novel Competition, was a resident artist at the Roundhouse in Camden and a Cityread Young Writer in Residence in Soho. She co-founded the Great Men project, which trains men to talk to teenage boys about gender equality and healthy relationships in school workshops, and has undertaken arts projects and community organising in gender issues and recovery/resilience after violence. Studying creative writing at Manchester Metropolitan University, she lives in Leeds and is currently working on her second novel.